FRIGHT NIGHT

ALSO BY MAREN STOFFELS

Escape Room

FRIGHT NIGHT

MAREN STOFFELS

TRANSLATED BY LAURA WATKINSON

Underlined

Text copyright © 2018 by Maren Stoffels
Cover art copyright © 2020 by Lauren Bates/Getty Images
Translation copyright © 2020 by Laura Watkinson

This publication has been made possible with financial support from the Dutch Foundation for Literature.

Nederlands letterenfonds
dutch foundation for literature

Visit us on the Web! GetUnderlined.com

Educators and librarians, for a variety of teaching tools, visit us at RHTeachersLibrarians.com

Library of Congress Cataloging-in-Publication Data
Names: Stoffels, Maren, author. | Watkinson, Laura, translator.
Title: Fright Night / Maren Stoffels ; translated by Laura Watkinson.
Other titles: Fright Night. English
Description: First edition. | New York : Underlined, [2020] | "Originally published in paperback by Leopold, Amsterdam in 2018." | Audience: Ages 12 and up. | Summary: "When a group of friends spends the night in a forest, they're confronted with their greatest fears. One of the friends won't survive the night. And one of them is a killer . . ." —Provided by publisher.
Identifiers: LCCN 2020013228 (print) | LCCN 2020013229 (ebook) | ISBN 978-0-593-17596-5 (trade paperback) | ISBN 978-0-593-17597-2 (ebook)
Subjects: CYAC: Murder—Fiction. | Fear—Fiction. | Forests and forestry—Fiction.
Classification: LCC PZ7.1.S7527 Fri 2020 (print) | LCC PZ7.1.S7527 (ebook) | DDC [Fic]—dc23

The text of this book is set in 12-point Adobe Garamond Pro.
Interior design by Ken Crossland

Printed in the United States of America
10 9 8 7 6 5 4 3 2 1
First Edition

For Nina. You were so brave to
tell your own story.
That meant I could write this story.
Thank you.

Maybe that's what happens
when a tornado meets a volcano

—Eminem

MURDERER

I always thought death would look different.
A bit like in the movies.
Spectacular, sad, or perhaps scary.
But your death was lonely,
even though there were four people around you:
three people watching—and me,
your murderer.

ONE HOUR BEFORE FRIGHT NIGHT

SOFIA

The three of us are riding our bikes in a line along the narrow bike path. The only illumination comes from our lights shining over the road.

The threatening words on that postcard have been on my mind all week. A few times I'd been on the verge of showing the card to Dylan, but I simply can't imagine the message is meant for him. Dylan doesn't have any enemies. Everyone at school likes him. There is no address on the card, so someone must have put it through the door in person. But who knows? Maybe it's just a silly joke.

"You excited?"

I look up. Dylan's cycling beside me, our handlebars almost touching. He's wearing a new pair of jeans and a T-shirt, and his eyes are shining. I try to imagine that he was ever seriously ill, but it's almost impossible.

"Yeah, sure."

Dylan smiles. "That doesn't sound very enthusiastic."

I actually have no idea what to think about this whole Fright Night business. My suggestion was just an impulse thing, because I wanted to do something with Quin and Dylan. Now that it's almost time, my nerves are really kicking in. It feels weird that I can't back out now. It's like the safety bars on the roller coaster have locked shut and the cars are slowly shunting along.

"Nearly there!" Quin points at a sign by the roadside. Someone had scrawled the words FRIGHT NIGHT on it.

"Feels like we're falling off the edge of the world," says Dylan.

"Then we must be in the right place."

I know Quin's right. The information they sent us said the woods were pretty remote, far from civilization. In the daytime, it's paradise for dog owners, who let their pets run free, but at night it's deserted.

We cycle up behind another boy and girl on bikes. The girl looks back and asks if we're here for Fright Night too.

"You bet," Quin says, bouncing up and down on his seat. All the way here, he's been listing exactly what he hopes to encounter in the woods. Dylan had looked at me and sighed a few times, and we both laughed. Quin can be so hyper.

A guy in a yellow vest is standing on the roadside with a flashlight in his hand. He signals at us to turn off the road. We see dozens of bike racks, and we quickly find places. Some other Fright Nighters are already walking around. Who are we going to get teamed up with? And what if we don't get along with them? We have to spend four hours together, so it could be a very long evening.

I run my fingers over the beads of my bracelet and try to

calm myself down. I remind myself that I'm with my friends, Dylan and Quin. I don't have to do this alone.

It's busy at the stand where we have to sign in. The two cyclists who arrived just before us join the line too.

"Some guys who did this last year told me they make you sign a contract," says Quin.

I look up in surprise. "What? Why?"

"We have to declare that we accept all responsibility for our participation. You know, just in case someone kicks the bucket."

I know Quin's joking, but I can still feel myself getting more and more nervous. Signing a contract sounds so . . . serious.

What have we gotten ourselves into?

FIVE DAYS BEFORE
FRIGHT NIGHT

DYLAN

"So what do you want to do this summer break?" Quin's lying on the bed with a book in his hands. He never reads, doesn't have the patience. My best friend always has to be talking. He spends half his classes out in the hallway because he stops everyone from working.

"Go swimming?"

I can't wait to be lying in the pool. Quin's attic room is so hot. I need to cool down.

My own bedroom, one floor below, is way less stuffy, but it still doesn't feel like mine. Quin's mom and dad have tried so hard to make me feel at home here. They bought a new bed and painted the walls. But I'd still rather sleep in Quin's room. On the extra mattress on the floor, I can pretend I'm just having a sleepover, like I used to.

But it isn't the way it used to be. I *live* here now, even though it sometimes feels like I just stole Quin's dad's study. Because of me, Johan has to work longer days at the office now. When I said that the other day, Quin immediately went on the defensive.

"What are you talking about? You're part of the family, Dylan. You always have been. It's just that it's official now."

I know that's how it is for Quin, but I still feel like an intruder in this family sometimes.

"Want to go to the pool tomorrow, then?" Quin gives me a cheeky grin. "I bet Sofia will want to come."

When I hear her name, I drop backward onto the mattress. I play with the key on the string around my neck.

The ceiling of Quin's room is made up of wooden boards. The cracks between them are the perfect place for secret messages. I always used to roll up notes and hide them there. It feels like centuries ago.

"Ow!"

A sharp pain shoots through my nose, right in the spot between my eyes. Then I see Quin's book lying beside me on the floor.

"What are you doing?" I yell. "You nearly broke my glasses!"

Quin grins. "I asked you a question. But you were just thinking about Sofia in a bikini, weren't you?"

Ever since Sofia joined our class at the start of this year, Quin has been making comments like that, each one more irritating than the last.

"Not everything is about Sofia," I say.

"Yeah. But a lot is." Suddenly Quin pounces on me. He grabs hold of my wrists and pushes them into the mattress. His face is just a few inches above mine.

"Admit it—you were thinking about her."

"Nope. I was thinking about the old days." I try to wriggle out of his grasp, but Quin bursts out laughing.

"It's about time you started lifting weights, my friend. Those arms of yours are pretty puny."

I try with all my might to push Quin off, but I can't. "Get off me!"

Quin shakes his head. "Not until you finally admit that you like Sofia."

"Then you'll just have to spend the rest of summer break sitting on me."

The door swings open. I expect to see Quin's mom, but instead of Hester, Sofia comes into the room. She's here so often that it's kind of like her second home.

Quin rolls off me and I sit up.

Sofia bursts out laughing. "Am I disturbing you guys?"

"Not at all," I say quickly. "What's up?"

Sofia drops down beside me on the mattress, and as always, I notice that she smells like she's just spent hours outside: fresh and sunny.

"You need to see this." Sofia unfolds a piece of paper. It looks like part of a poster; the edges are torn and some of the words are missing.

Quin chuckles. "Did you tear that off a noticeboard on the way over here?"

Sofia smooths out the paper. "Yup."

"What is it?" I ask.

"An ad for Fright Night."

"For what?"

"Your chance to put an end to your fears forever."

I reach for the arms of my glasses and push them more snugly onto my face. *Put an end to your fears.* Sofia's words buzz around inside my head. Imagine if that were possible. I could finally sleep at night, and the bad memories would be a thing of the past.

"Fears? I don't have any," says Quin.

"BS. Everyone gets scared sometimes." Sofia looks at me. Her green eyes warm me and freeze me at the same time. "What's your biggest fear?"

The question takes me by surprise. It feels like the room is slowly changing into a different one. A room with blue linoleum on the floor. I feel the needles going into my arm again, sometimes as many as five in one day. Bloodwork, IV drips, checking levels of this and that. I couldn't keep count.

"Heights," I say, making something up. "You guys want something to drink?"

Sofia nods. "Yeah. Orange soda?"

"Me too," says Quin.

I get up off the mattress. My right leg protests as usual, and I almost trip over Sofia when I step across her. As soon as I close the door behind me, I pause on the landing. It feels like I'm wearing a tie that's way too tight.

I need some fresh air. I head down the steep attic stairs and throw open the door to my own room. It's dark in here. Out of habit, I still keep the curtains closed. I pull them aside and open the balcony doors.

The fresh air comes streaming into my room, and I drop onto the floor and lie down. I feel the wooden floor under the back of my head. It makes me feel calm—there's no sign of any blue linoleum.

Your chance to put an end to your fears forever.

Sofia sounded so positive when she said it, like she really believes it. I remember an article I read recently, about people with phobias. It said it sometimes helps people to get over their fear if you expose them to it. It made me think about Hester's suggestion that I try eye movement desensitization and reprocessing therapy. The therapist takes you back to the moments when you experienced a traumatic event that now causes stress or anxiety, and you relive them, processing the feelings associated with them in a safe setting. Just the thought of it made me shudder. Why would I want to go through all those moments again?

But maybe this Fright Night could work. Maybe I need to be really scared for a night so that I can put my fears into perspective.

I look at my new bed. I've hardly slept in it. Quin's snoring really gets on my nerves, but at the same time I need it to fall asleep. As long as Quin is snoring, everything is fine and I can feel safe.

The first night in this room, I woke up screaming. Hester and Johan rushed in and sat on the edge of my bed for a while. Hester's face was pale with worry, and I felt so ashamed that I'd given them such a fright. But I also know that I can't sleep in Quin's room for the rest of my life. There'll come a time when I have to cope on my own. And maybe that time has come.

I stand up slowly and head to the kitchen, where Hester is cooking dinner. At first I thought Quin's family only had such great dinners when I was visiting, but since I moved in, I know they have meals like that every night.

"Can I get a drink?"

Hester looks up and smiles. "You know you don't have to ask every time now."

Yeah, it's such an irritating habit. I quickly open the fridge so she won't see my red cheeks.

"Having fun upstairs?"

"Yeah, sure."

"She's a nice girl, that Sofia."

Hester's as bad as Quin. She's never actually said so, but I know she thinks the two of us are a good match.

"Dylan?"

I take three glasses from the cabinet. "Yes?"

"You can trust her."

I know what Hester's trying to say. She thinks I should talk to Sofia and Quin about what happened.

Johan and Hester have told Quin only half the story, because I don't want anything to change between us. My best friend knows just enough to understand why I'm living here, but he hasn't asked me anything otherwise. And I don't know what I'd do if he suddenly started asking me questions. Where would I start?

"I know."

"At your own pace," says Hester. "Okay?"

I nod and quickly head upstairs with three glasses and a

bottle of orange soda. Hester's giving me time, but she still brings it up pretty often. I know she's right. It's not good that Quin's the only one in the house who doesn't know the whole story, but I can't bring myself to tell him the truth. It could change everything between us, and I don't want that to happen. I want to be his friend, not some kind of patient.

At Quin's bedroom door, I take a deep breath and then open it. The heat billows into my face again.

"Where did you get to? I'm dying of thirst." Quin snatches the bottle from my hand and fills the glasses.

"Here's to summer break," says Sofia, raising her glass.

"And to Fright Night," Quin adds. "A night in the woods, facing our greatest fears. It sounds perfect."

It sounds like hours of EMDR therapy, but this is a much better and more exciting alternative. Plus, I don't have to do it alone. There are three of us.

"You sure you're up for it?" asks Sofia.

"Sure." I nod. "Bring it on."

"This is going to be so cool." Sofia puts her arms around me. Before I realize what's happening, I feel her body against mine. We've never been this close before and her hair tickles my cheek. Startled, I splash soda over the edge of my glass.

"I'm going to sign us up right now," Quin says, grabbing his laptop.

Inside my head, I can hear Hester's voice. *You can trust her.*

SOFIA

Dylan's body freezes as soon as I touch him. I instantly let go, but it doesn't improve the sense of distance between us. Even worse, it makes me feel more distant from him than ever.

"We need a team of five," says Quin. "Or we can't take part. If we sign up as a team of three, the organizers will match us up with another group that doesn't have enough players."

Fright Night with strangers? I know Dylan won't like that idea. Quin's the one who's always up for a challenge. Dylan prefers to stay in the background. At school, whole recesses go by without him saying anything. It's barely noticeable, though, because Quin talks enough for two.

"Let's do it," Dylan suddenly says, much to my surprise. First he agreed to Fright Night and now he'll do it with strangers? I don't get it.

"We're just in time—today's the last day to sign up."

I go stand by Quin and look at the screen with him. "Do we have to give them any details?"

Quin points. "They want to know our greatest fears. Are they going to use them against us later?"

I think back to the beginning of this school year. I was new at school and didn't know anyone. I've never been more afraid, but Fright Night probably can't do anything with that. Maybe I should put down insects. I hate creepy-crawlies with their tickly little feet.

"How long does this Fright Night last?" asks Dylan.

"Four hours." Quin is beaming. "I can't wait."

I read through the information. They have actors who do all kinds of stuff to scare you. And special "Scare Zones"—each with a different theme. That's where the actors take things "a step further." What's that supposed to mean?

Dylan installs himself on his mattress again and picks a book up off the floor. He says heights are his greatest fear, but I have a feeling he came up with that on the spot.

If I were him, I'd mostly be scared of something happening to my mom. He visits his mom every Sunday, and she's too sick to take care of him. That's why he's been living at Quin's for a year now.

I don't know exactly what's wrong with Dylan's mom. He's not much of a talker, and I've never wanted to pry. Maybe my greatest fear is that I'll drive him away, like just now with the hug.

Very occasionally Dylan takes a small step toward me, like when it was my last birthday and he came up with the perfect gift: a bracelet with blue-green beads. "The stone's called aquamarine," he said as I took the bracelet out of the box. "It's supposed to make you happy, relaxed, and carefree."

I looked up. "You think I need that?"

"Maybe just a bit."

I knew he was talking about the first few weeks of this school year. Dylan was the first one to speak to me, at the school dance. Could he see just how scared I was?

I fiddle with the beads on my wrist. I haven't taken off the bracelet since he gave it to me. In every new situation, it reminds me to be confident. It's Dylan's birthday soon, and for a while I've been trying to come up with a gift that will live up to his.

I look at Dylan, who's leafing through the book. He reads more—and faster—than Quin and me put together. A deep line appears between his eyebrows whenever he's concentrating on something. The old-fashioned round glasses he wears look like something from the 1960s, but they really suit him. His short, dark hair is messy, and there's a small birthmark on his cheek in the shape of a half-moon.

Around his neck is a key on a worn-out cord. The first time I saw what was on the cord was when we were at the pool one time. I have no idea what the key's for.

As Dylan moves his right leg, the line between his eyebrows becomes deeper. I think it hurts him more often than he lets on. In gym class, he sometimes drags it behind him like a pirate with a wooden leg. He fell off his bike when he was a kid, and the fracture never healed properly.

I stand up. "I'm just going to the bathroom."

One floor down, it's a lot cooler than in the attic, and I take a few big gulps of oxygen. Then I notice that the door to Dylan's room is open a crack. There's a poster of his favorite band on the wall. Why do we never spend time in Dylan's room? We always hang out in Quin's attic.

I've never been in Dylan's room before. Curious, I push the door open a little more. There's not much furniture in there, just the essentials. A bed, a big wardrobe, and a desk with piles of schoolbooks. I step through the doorway. Are there no pictures of his mom anywhere? I'm interested to see what she looks like and if Dylan looks like her. But other than the poster, I don't see any personal details in the room.

Suddenly a great idea for a gift comes to me. Maybe I can make a photo album with Dylan's memories in it. Quin can help. He's known him so long. And maybe Hester has some photos of Dylan from when he was little.

I run my hand over the desktop. So this is where Dylan does his homework. Does he ever think about his old house? That makes me think about mine. It was beautiful, surrounded by meadows and cows, but then Dad got a promotion, so we had to move. I felt so miserable and lonely here at first, but at least I still had my mom and dad.

Dylan had to start all over again almost a year ago, in a new house, with a new family. Maybe that was why he sensed he should come over to me at the school dance. I open the door of Dylan's wardrobe. My eye instantly falls on his pressed button-down shirt, the one he was wearing that night. Does he remember our first conversation as well as I do? I bring the sleeve of Dylan's shirt up to my nose and smell it for a moment.

I hear a sound downstairs. Startled, I let go of the shirt.

What am I doing?! I don't have Dylan's permission. It's like I'm secretly reading his diary. If someone snooped around *my* room without asking, I'd be so mad at them.

I quickly shut the wardrobe door and go downstairs. In the kitchen, Quin's mom looks up from the counter.

"Sofia, are you staying for dinner? I made extra."

That's so typical of Quin's mom—she wants to take care of everyone. I'm not surprised they took Dylan into their home. He could have done a lot worse.

"I'd love to another time, but I have homework to do."

Hester sighs. "I wish Quin would follow your example. He hasn't done any homework since Dylan moved in. They get up to all kinds of things in that attic, but homework's not one of them."

I smile. "I bet it's not."

Shall I ask her about the photos now? Dylan's birthday is at the end of next week. I need to hurry.

"Can I ask you something?"

Hester nods. "Sure."

"Do you have any old photos of Dylan?"

Hester looks up in surprise. "Why do you ask?"

"I want to make a photo album for his birthday."

"What a nice idea." Hester beams at me. "Sure, I have some photos of him. I'll get out the photo boxes later."

"And I want to take some pictures of his old street."

There's a brief silence.

"His old street?"

"Sometimes I really miss my old place. You know, the little

22

things, like the baker on the corner, and the cool view from my bedroom window."

"Yeah . . ." Hester stirs the food in the pan. "Yeah, sure."

Why do I feel like I said something wrong?

"Do you have the address?" I ask tentatively.

"Of course. Give me a moment." Hester pulls a sheet of paper from a notepad and writes something on it. "There you go. It's a really sweet idea. I'll get the photos out for you before you go."

KELLY

Where is he? I look down the street again, but there's no sign of Sandy. The grocery store isn't far from our housing complex. He just went to fetch some cigarettes, that's all.

Sandy. The first time I heard his name, I thought it was a girl. But, of course, most people think Kelly's a girl's name, too, even though it's short for Kelvin in my case. Two boys with names that can be girls' names—an inseparable duo.

I look at my watch. Sandy's been away for over half an hour. I twist a long strand of hair around my index finger. Every inch my hair grows takes me farther away from the past.

"Hurry up, man."

"You waiting for someone?"

I turn and find myself looking into Nell's face. As always, I can't seem to breathe properly when I'm around her. She's bleached her hair again and it's kind of glowing in the sunshine.

"Sandy's taking his time again," I say.

Nell pats the bench beside her. "If you have to wait, you might as well sit here."

Recently we've been spending more time together. Nell

comes and talks to me when I'm alone, and I do the same with her. Whenever we eat as a group, she always sits next to me. Even Sandy's started to notice. I drop down onto the bench and Nell takes a cigarette out of her inside pocket.

"Want one of mine?"

I gratefully accept. "How did you know I needed this?"

"Your hands." Nell takes my hand and lifts it up between our faces. "You're totally shaking."

I look at her fingers, with the familiar rings on them. One on each finger, except for her ring finger.

"For my wedding ring one day," Nell says when she sees me looking. She lets go of my hand and it falls back onto the bench. It's like I can still feel her touch.

"But that's a long way off, getting married. Need to find a boyfriend first."

Deep inside, my hope's burning away like a campfire. I've been trying to find out for months if she has someone, and now she's gone and told me herself.

Sometimes it's like Nell forgets she's a neighbor instead of a friend. Neighbors—that's what they call the volunteers who live around our complex. They're there to make us feel as ordinary as possible and to help us eventually return to "normal society." Strangely, though, the neighbors have exactly the opposite effect on me. Every day they just serve to remind me that I'm some kind of special case.

Unless I'm with Nell. I often have the idea that she feels the same way about me as I do about her. Or is that just because it's what I want to see?

Nell takes a drag on her cigarette and leans back with a sigh. "What's your excuse for smoking?"

I shrug. "It's just this filthy habit I have."

"That's not true. Everyone starts for a reason."

"Sandy," I say. "Sandy was my reason."

"Did you want to play tough for him?"

I think back to the moment we met. A gang of boys was hassling me, and Sandy stuck up for me. As usual, with his fists. After the fight, we both sat outside on a wall in the sunshine. Our bloody noses were slowly drying up, and Sandy took out a packet of tobacco.

"Here." Sandy rolled a cigarette and gave it to me. "Now you belong."

"To what?" I asked.

"To the club."

"Who's in the club?"

"Me."

"And who else?"

"You."

I smile at the memory. A club of two. We don't need any other members.

"Sandy's a bad influence on you," says Nell, which makes her sound like a neighbor.

"He's okay."

"The two of you are so different."

"You think?"

"Yes, Sandy is so . . . intense."

I smile. "Yeah, that's a good word to describe him."

"And you're . . ."

I look at Nell from the side. She bites her bottom lip, and I have to fight the urge to kiss her.

"Normal," Nell decides.

I burst out laughing. "Normal?!"

"I think so."

Is that really what she thinks about me? The hope inside me flares up again.

"We really should quit," says Nell, taking another drag on her cigarette. "Smoking, I mean."

We. Nell and me. Together.

"Then why don't we?" Recklessly, I pluck the cigarette from between Nell's lips and toss it to the ground. I send my own cigarette flying after.

"There."

We both look at the cigarettes, smoldering on the paving stones.

"My dad will be so grateful to you. He hates that I smoke," Nell says with a smile. "What about yours?"

"He's dead."

Nell curses. "Sorry, I didn't know."

"How would you know?" I say. "Both my parents died in a car accident. Killed instantly."

"Is that why you live here?" asks Nell.

I can feel the nerves in my body, like I always do whenever this subject comes up. Sandy knows about it, and my psychologists, but no one else. Can I confide in Nell? Maybe I should try. It could bring us closer together. And Nell's different from all the other neighbors around here.

"I did something because of anger, because of hate. I destroyed someone's life because I thought I had every right to."

Silence. Is Nell going to run away after all? Honesty sucks. The silence just hangs in the air, making me nervous.

"Go on. Leave," I say.

Nell looks up. Her cheeks are flushed red. "Why?"

I squeeze out a smile. "Because now you know I'm not that normal after all."

Nell shakes her head and looks at the cigarettes on the ground. "We've all done stuff we're not proud of."

...

"I'm back!" The door of our room flies open and Sandy's standing there.

I tear my eyes away from the empty bench outside, where I was just sitting with Nell. Her words are still echoing through my mind. She actually reacted really well. Maybe one day I can tell her the whole truth.

"Where *were* you?" I look at my watch. "You've been gone for over an hour!"

"Bumped into someone." Sandy throws the pack of cigarettes onto my comforter. I automatically start to open it, but then I stop and toss it into the trash can.

"What are you doing?"

28

"Quitting," I say. "As of today."

"Why?" Sandy takes the pack out of the trash.

"It's bad for you."

"Loads of stuff is bad for you." Sandy puts the cigarettes into his pocket and shrugs. "But great, all the more for me."

"So who'd you bump into?"

Sandy looks at me. "What?"

"You said you bumped into someone. Who was it?"

"Oh." Sandy makes a dismissive gesture. "Just someone I used to know."

He takes a lanyard with a pass attached out of his bag and throws it onto my lap. "This is for you."

"What is it?" I turn the pass around in my fingers. On one side, there's a picture of a horror clown, with the dates of the next six weekends. On the other side, I read in big letters: FRIGHT NIGHT.

"Are we going to this?"

"No, dummy, they're our staff passes. We're going to work there!" Sandy grins. "And we are going to make big bucks."

I let his words sink in. What the hell was Sandy thinking?

"I sent in our names a while back. We start on Saturday morning. There's a training session that finishes at four. And Fright Night kicks off at midnight."

So he did all this behind my back? He often takes the lead, but this is going too far.

"Why didn't you say anything?"

Sandy sighs. "Because I knew you'd give me a hard time about it, like you are now."

"I'm not giving you a hard time. I just—"

Sandy raises his hand. "Before you continue, let me tell you how much we're going to make."

When he tells me the amount, I actually feel my jaw drop. I've never had that much money in my entire life. When I think of all the things I could do with it . . .

Sandy gives me a satisfied nod. "So you're convinced, then?"

I shrug. "Depends. What exactly do we have to do at this training session?"

"Oh, it's a load of BS. They think they have to teach us how to scare people, but I'm sure you and I are going to be naturals. We'll make people so terrified they'll never dare sleep again."

Sandy kicks off his shoes and drops down onto his bed. We could have gotten separate rooms, but we've been living together for so long that we just left it that way. I see that he's turning his own pass in his hand now. His eyes are gleaming. I bet he's already coming up with ways to drive the Fright Nighters insane.

I glance at the burn on his right hand. Sandy likes to tell girls a heroic story about rescuing someone from a burning house, but I know what really happened. I know Sandy's stories and he knows mine.

As I look at the pass again, I feel a wave of energy go through my body. The two of us know more than anyone what fear is. This job was made for us.

SOFIA

I brake in front of the corner house, number 12. The rental places in this neighborhood all look the same, green front doors with yellow glass. I don't know exactly what I was expecting, but it's a huge contrast with Quin's street, where the houses are much bigger and fancier.

Is Dylan's mom home? I don't see any movement through the downstairs window, and the curtains upstairs are closed. Cautiously, I take a few photos of the front yard and the house.

I press the doorbell. Three notes ring through the hallway, and I feel my hands sweating. What kind of woman is Dylan's mom? I just hope she thinks my gift's a good idea, like Hester does.

"Hey, there's no one home, you know."

The voice makes me jump, and I turn around. A boy of about ten is standing in front of me, with a soccer ball in his hands.

"Are you Dylan's girlfriend?"

I smile. "I'm just a friend."

"Dylan doesn't live here anymore." The boy bounces the ball a few times. "But we always used to play soccer together."

Then he looks at my camera. "You taking photos?"

I nod. "I'm making a book for Dylan's birthday. Can I take a picture of you too?"

The boy nods and does a tough-guy pose for me. As I'm taking the photo, I hear someone call, "Sven!"

"That's me. Got to go. Dinner." The boy waves. "Bye."

I look at the result. The photo's perfect, with the street in the background. If I can keep this up, I'll soon have a great gift for Dylan. The idea makes me happy, and I walk down the path beside Dylan's house. It leads to an overgrown backyard full of stinging nettles.

On a patio, there's a rusty swing and a plastic picnic table with a big puddle on it from yesterday's rainstorm. That's another difference from Quin's place, where they have a huge set of lounge furniture in the backyard.

I take some pictures, but the results are as sad as it looks in real life. I place my hands on the glass of the patio doors and peer inside. I can see the living room and part of the kitchen. Should I take some photos through the glass? I lift my camera and immediately lower it. This is going too far—I'm not a paparazzo.

"Are you looking for someone?"

I turn around. There's an older gray-haired woman standing behind me, with a bunch of keys in her hand. Is she Dylan's mom? He looks nothing like her.

"I . . . I'm Sofia, a friend of Dylan's."

"Aha." The woman smiles when she hears his name. "My little guy. How's he doing?"

So it's not his mom, but then who is she?

"Gerda." The woman holds out her hand. "I'm the neighbor. Trying to keep the place spick-and-span until Liane gets back."

So Dylan's mom doesn't live here anymore. Is she in the hospital?

Gerda looks curiously at my camera. "So what are you doing here?"

"I'm making a gift for Dylan. It's his birthday soon. He has hardly any photos in his new bedroom, so I thought it might be nice to make a photo album full of different memories. Would you mind if I took a picture of you too?"

The woman blushes. "Sure. Go ahead."

I take a couple of quick pictures, and I'm about to leave when Gerda nods at the house.

"Want to take some pictures inside too?"

I look up in surprise. "Am I allowed?"

"Sure. For Dylan's birthday, everything's allowed." Gerda puts a key in the back door and unlocks it.

Before I know what's happening, I'm in the kitchen. Under one of the magnets on the fridge, there's a grocery list in Dylan's handwriting.

"Dylan could use a friend like you after everything that happened." Gerda takes a bucket out of the sink cabinet and turns on the faucet. "It's terrible, what he went through. All that time in bed—no child should have to suffer like that."

33

It's a moment before the words really sink in.

"Huh? Was Dylan sick?"

"Didn't you know?"

This doesn't make sense. His mom is the one in the hospital, isn't she?

"I only met Dylan this year," I say. "And he's not much of a talker."

"That's true enough. They're similar like that." Gerda points at my camera. "Go on, knock yourself out."

"Yeah . . . great. Thanks."

I'm trying to pull myself together, but it's not easy. Why didn't Dylan ever tell me anything? If I'm to believe Gerda, he was really sick. Was it the same sickness as his mom?

I take photos of the round dining table with the three chairs, the piano, and the big sofa. The place looks spotless, like Gerda mops and polishes everything daily.

"So you're new around here?" I hear Gerda ask from the kitchen.

"We moved here at the beginning of this school year."

"How do you like it?"

"Well, it's fine now, but not so much at first," I admit.

"Why's that?"

"I felt pretty . . ."

"Lonely?" Gerda comes out of the kitchen with the bucket in her hand. "I know the feeling. When I came to live here, I thought I was going crazy."

I smile. "Something like that, yes. But Dylan helped me.

He spoke to me at our school dance. It was like he realized that I was really miserable."

"Takes after his mother. She did the same for me. Liane's a pretty private person, but she always had time for a chat with me. Such a caring woman."

I run my fingers over the beads of my bracelet and look around. What else can I take photos of?

Then I notice the windowsill. Half hidden behind the curtain, there's a photo frame. I pull it out and find myself looking into the faces of a dark-haired woman—and Dylan. He must have been about ten, but I still recognize him. He's not wearing glasses yet and he's looking kind of awkwardly into the camera, like it's the first time anyone's ever taken a photo of him.

Why didn't Dylan bring this photo for his room? I'd have thought he'd want to have a photo of his mom.

"Why don't you take it with you?" I hear Gerda say behind me.

"Are you sure?"

"Yes, it'll be fine." She goes on cleaning.

I take the photo from the frame and slip it into the inside pocket of my denim jacket before walking out into the hallway. There's a big pile of mail on the doormat, all addressed to *L. Dumont,* Dylan's mom. I sweep it up and am about to put the stack on the cupboard in the hallway when I spot a postcard.

The blue lake on the front is close to where I used to live. When my friends and I had some free time, we often went swimming there.

"Oh, that was their favorite vacation spot." Gerda has appeared behind me again. "You should take that postcard for him too."

I nod and put it into my pocket with the photo. My gaze shifts to the stairs. Dylan's bedroom must be up there.

"I don't know if Liane will like you going upstairs," says Gerda. "That's maybe a bit too private."

Fine by me. I already have the most important thing: a photo of Dylan and his mom.

Gerda opens the front door for me, and I wave goodbye. "Bye! And thanks for your help!"

"You're welcome. Come by another time. And say hello to Dylan for me, won't you?"

●●●

At home, I look at the photos on my camera. They've turned out well. I even cycled over to Dylan's old elementary school to take photos of the schoolyard. He was probably at that school when he got sick. I'd like to ask Dylan about it, but there must be a reason why he hasn't told me anything.

I count the photos. There are lots of them, particularly when you include Hester's selection. Dylan's mom is smiling a bit cagily in the photo, the way Dylan sometimes does. He doesn't often give a big grin, but when he does it's like he's saved that smile just for me.

Then I take the postcard out of the inside pocket of my denim jacket, which is hanging on the back of my desk chair.

I look at the lake on the front of the postcard again. It's crazy to think we've both been there, but not together. I know why Dylan and his mom liked to go there. It's such an awesome place.

Who sent Dylan this card? When I turn it over, I have to read the words three times before they sink in. They just don't go with that sunny vacation picture.

ONE DAY I'M GOING TO KILL YOU.

JUST BEFORE
FRIGHT NIGHT

MURDERER

That was the time to say: *I'm not doing it.*
I'm not going with you into the woods.
If I'd done that, everything would have turned out differently.
And you would still be alive.

DYLAN

Outside, it's slowly getting dark. Not long now before Fright Night begins. Quin's chattering is driving me crazy, so I've retreated to my own room. The comforter is still perfectly clean. I've slept in Quin's room all week, as usual. I didn't dare to sleep here, too scared of nightmares. But after tonight, everything is going to be different. Soon I'll sleep in this room, on my own.

I look down at the shorts I'm wearing. My crooked right leg looks even worse in shorts. Maybe I should wear something else tonight. I stand up to open my wardrobe, but then I notice that the door is ajar. As soon as I open the door, I see what the problem is: the sleeve of my only good shirt is sticking out.

How did that happen? Hang on. It can't have been Sofia, can it? I haven't worn the thing for ages. Maybe Hester hung something in my wardrobe. I can't imagine she did that, though. The first week I lived here, I got really stressed out because of all the changes, and Hester realized pretty quickly what was going on. When she asked what she could do to help me, I said I wanted to put away my own clothes.

She burst out laughing and said, "Wish I had another son like you!" She didn't mean anything by it, but it still sounded strange, a bit like she was trying to take Mom's place.

I look at the shirt. Maybe Quin wanted to borrow something from my wardrobe. But he has his own style—he likes loud prints and thinks my clothes are boring. Anyway, there are enough of my clothes in his room already.

I take the shirt out of the wardrobe and think back to the school dance. That was the night I got to know Sofia, the night I finally dared to approach her. Quin was sick that night, so no one would go on about it forever and ever if my attempt was a failure.

"Beautiful"—that was the first thing I said. I was talking about Sofia's dress, and it sounded so dumb I could have bitten off my tongue. But Sofia just smiled.

"I hate dresses," she said.

"Me too."

That made both of us laugh. When she stayed with me for the rest of the night, I felt invincible.

I hold the shirt against me and close my eyes for a moment.

"You ready? Time to go." Quin is standing in the doorway, eyebrows raised. "What are you doing now?"

I quickly lower the shirt. "Nothing."

"You going to wear that tonight?"

I shake my head. "Of course not."

"Nervous, huh?"

"A bit," I confess.

"Because Sofia's coming with us?"

43

I sigh. Quin tries it every single day, no matter what I say or do.

"No need to answer." Quin grins. "I can see straight through you."

Dr. Savory looks at me with a question on her face. "Where exactly does it hurt?"

She isn't like the doctors I've met before. Dr. Savory has a sparkle in her eyes when she talks to me.

I hesitate.

"The doctor asked you a question, honey." My mom is in her usual place behind the doctor. "And it won't do anyone any good if you lie."

I tense all the muscles in my face and make what I call my poop face. I raise my arm a very short way off the mattress and then, panting, I let it fall.

"My arms hurt," I say quietly. "And my legs."

The doctor nods. "We'll do some bloodwork, so we can rule out a few things."

More bloodwork? How many needles have I had in my arm? I'm like a pincushion.

"It'll be fine, honey," I hear Mom's soft voice say. "Just be brave."

When Quin closes my door behind him, his words linger in my room. Quin thinks he knows me better than anyone, but he only knows half the truth. Will he be hurt if he finds out?

44

Maybe. I just don't know if I can ever tell him about those memories.

And what about Sofia? I haven't known her nearly as long, but sometimes I feel so close to her. Like on Monday, when she suddenly threw her arms around me in Quin's room. Although I really want her close, it's better to keep her at a distance. The farther people are from me, the less they can see.

I hang the shirt back up and close the wardrobe door. This time it shuts perfectly.

KELLY

"The safe word for Fright Night is *ketchup*."

There's laughter around us, but the man who's running the training course looks so serious that the laughter abruptly ceases.

"If the Fright Nighters use that word, you have to stop immediately. Is that clear?"

The trainer pauses to let the words sink in. There are a lot of us here. Fright Night is a big event, with more than a hundred people taking part. Most of the actors are students, a bit older than Sandy and me. But some of them are professional actors who do these kinds of events all the time.

Soon we'll all have makeup put on and they're going to give us scary costumes. I can't wait to see what I'm going to look like tonight.

A girl in front of me puts up her hand. "And what do we do if they beg us to stop? Do we stop then too?"

The trainer shakes his head. "That's going to happen all the time. We're here to scare people. It's what they paid for, guys."

I glance at Sandy next to me. He has a slight smile on his

face. He was one of the best in the training session. Even some of the professionals were impressed. The girl Sandy had to practice on turned white as a sheet. I actually forgot it was just Sandy.

"If any of the Fright Nighters pass out or become unwell, use the walkie-talkie to call the first-aid station." The trainer holds up a black device with a few knobs and an antenna. "Every group will have one."

"Why can't we just use our cell phones?" someone asks.

The trainer smiles. "That'd be a neat trick. There's no signal anywhere in the woods."

SOFIA

It's busy at the stand where we have to sign in for Fright Night. I see Quin looking curiously at the sheet of paper listing the groups. I hope the two other Fright Nighters in our group are cool.

"We've been put in a group with a guy called Martin de Vries and—"

"That's us," I hear behind me. I turn around to see the couple who were cycling in front of us.

"Martin." The boy gives me a firm handshake. He looks a bit older than us. He has a ginger beard, freckles, and must be at least a head taller than me. If it gets too scary later, I can always hide behind him.

"Sofia," I say.

The girl gives me a softer handshake. Her eyes are friendly, and I have a sudden sense that I can trust her, like I've known her for a long time. The nerves I was just feeling have vanished.

"Sofia," I say with a relieved grin. These two seem to be okay.

"Hi, Sofia." The girl smiles. "I'm Nell."

DYLAN

My right leg is starting to hurt. That has been happening a lot recently, whenever I have to stand for a long time. I look at Nell and Sofia, who appear to be getting along. They're chatting away like they've been friends for years.

Sofia seems less tense. On the bike she looked a bit pale, but now she's more at ease. I smile when I see the bracelet on her wrist. Does she wear it every day? I was so nervous about the gift. It felt like I was giving her something silly and insignificant, but I really wanted to buy it with my own money, without being a burden on Hester and Johan.

At the end of next week, it's my turn for a birthday, the first one without Mom. Hester's trying everything she can to give me a fun day, but her efforts are actually making it kind of awkward. I don't need any cake or loads of visitors and gifts. What I'd really like to do is disappear and resurface the next day.

"Last year there was a box with, like, twelve hundred crickets inside, and the Fright Nighters had to dig around in it with their hands," I hear Martin say.

"Seriously?" Sofia grimaces. "That's a joke, right?"

"I swear."

"Stop it." Nell gives Martin a prod. "You're just getting everyone all worked up."

"What? It's true."

"Twelve hundred crickets." Quin laughs and nudges me. "That's so sick, huh?"

I nod. "Yeah, totally sick."

"Your son's blood is healthy."

It feels like my hospital bed is turning into a swampy marsh.

"Healthy?" Mom's voice shoots up an octave. "How is that possible?"

"We found no abnormalities," Dr. Savory explains.

"But . . . Dylan says it feels like the world is spinning! He fell over in the kitchen the other day because he couldn't keep his balance. And now you're telling me he's healthy?"

"I'm saying his blood is healthy," the doctor corrects her.

Mom shakes her head. "You need to keep looking. I know there's something wrong with him."

"Names?"

It's finally our turn. Quin lists our names. The man at the desk nods and crosses all five of us off the list.

"Great. Your group's complete, so now you can fill out the contracts and hand them in over there." He points at another desk.

I take the sheet of letter paper. Quin was right. There really is a contract. Isn't that totally over the top? I take the contract over to one of the standing tables, where Quin immediately starts frantically checking all the boxes. Sofia's biting the end of her pen.

I focus on my own contract and start reading.

Dear Fright Nighter,

As organizers, we would like to ask you to read the following points carefully.

Check the boxes to indicate that you have read and understood the warnings.

❏ I understand that Fright Night can be disturbing and intense.

❏ I understand that my freedom of movement may be severely restricted at times.

❏ I understand that the actors have to stop at all times if I use the safe word KETCHUP. In that case, Fright Night will end immediately for my group.

During Fright Night, it is not
permitted to:

❑ Take photographs or make video
  recordings.
❑ Make use of flashlights that you
  have brought here yourself.
❑ Touch our actors.
❑ Eat, drink, or smoke.
❑ Carry sharp objects, such as
  umbrellas.

Fright Night is not suitable for
anyone:
❑ Who is under the age of sixteen.
❑ Who has heart problems.
❑ Who has epilepsy.
❑ Who suffers from claustrophobia.
❑ Who is pregnant.
❑ Who can't stand the sight of
  blood.
❑ Who is unable to walk
  independently.

Access to Fright Night is permitted
only with a valid admission ticket
and after this contract has been
signed.

```
I understand and accept that the
organizers of Fright Night are in no
way liable for any kind of damage
(either physical or emotional)
suffered by me as a result of
participation in Fright Night.

First and last names:
Date of birth:
Today's date:
Signature:
```

"Why do you think we're not allowed to touch the actors?" Sofia has chewed the end of her pen to pieces. My own pen is still hovering over the dotted line.

"They must be worried that people will just lash out as a reflex," says Quin. He snatches my contract. "Where's your signature?"

"I still need to sign." I take back my contract. "Lash out? What do you mean?"

"Simple. If someone scares you, what do you do?"

"Run away," replies Sofia before I can say anything.

"I don't know," I say. "Nothing, I think."

"Just my luck," Quin says with a sigh. "I'm out for a night with Ms. Flight and Mr. Fright."

"Mr. what now?"

"Everyone reacts differently when they're in danger." Quin puts up three fingers. "You've got flight: the people who run away as soon as they get the chance, heading for safety. Then there's fright: the ones who don't do anything but just freeze. And then there are the fighters. They face the situation head-on—and they use their fists."

"So that makes you Mr. Fight, right?" Sofia says, giving Quin's skinny upper arm a squeeze. "Hmm, I'm curious to see how that works out."

Quin pouts and looks offended. "You just wait. Want to bet you'll be begging to hide behind my big broad back before long?"

Sofia and I both burst out laughing. Now that Quin's standing next to Martin, it's even more obvious just how small he is.

Quin points at my dotted line. "Go on, Mr. Fright, sign it. Or I'll do it for you."

KELLY

"Shit, man. You are one hot mess."

It *is* Sandy. I know that because I was sitting next to him the entire time with the makeup artist, but when I see him here in the dark woods, shivers run down my spine. They've turned him into a sort of horror clown, with long, sharp teeth. He's wearing yellow contact lenses, which gleam when I aim the flashlight at him.

"No, dude. You're the hot stuff around here!" says Sandy.

The makeup was applied in thick layers, and they just kept smearing it on. When I saw the result in the mirror, I couldn't believe it was me looking back. A face covered in scars, with deep furrows and lines. They blackened some of my teeth so it looks like I have big gaping holes in my mouth.

The only giveaway is my eyes. I took out the contacts they gave me as soon as I could because they stung so bad.

"We're going to move soon. This spot is lame."

The organizers put us close to the start of Fright Night. I can hear the music at the entrance from behind our wall.

55

"I want to do more than just jump out and scare people. Don't you?"

I know exactly what Sandy means. The professional actors, who have done Fright Night before, are in the four Scare Zones. They go way beyond just scaring people. They push the Fright Nighters to the limits. The words *Insect Zone* gave me the shivers. The video of the twelve hundred crickets from last year has been burned into my memory since the training, and someone said they were actually live.

Why would anyone volunteer for this? I don't think the Fright Nighters have any idea what's waiting for them in these woods.

"As soon as the first groups have passed, we'll set off. We're the best, Kelly. Staying here is a waste of our talents. I want to unleash the insects on the Fright Nighters. I want to lock them up. I want to drive them insane!"

I shake my head. "I don't want to get fired on the first night."

"Don't be a sap. No one's going to notice." Sandy takes something out of his pocket. "And there's always this . . ."

I see something glint in the beam of our flashlight and step back, startled.

"What the . . . ?!"

"A knife, what'd you think?"

"But we're not allowed to have sharp objects!"

When did Sandy put that thing in his pocket? I didn't notice anything at all!

"That rule only applies to the Fright Nighters," says Sandy.

"Anyway, there's one guy out there with a baton and there's a girl with a chainsaw!"

I look at the knife in Sandy's hand. It's a switchblade, the kind of knife that shoots out of the handle when you press a button. Is it the same knife that got him into trouble before?

"Put it away," I say. "Please."

"You're so paranoid." Sandy puts the knife in the pocket of his clown suit. "I'm not going to stab anyone."

Suddenly I remember Nell's words: *Sandy's a bad influence on you.* Sandy might seem intense, but in reality he wouldn't harm a fly now. Sure he's done things he shouldn't have, but he's calmed down a lot. He hasn't been in a fight for a few months, and he's being a good boy and going to all his therapy sessions. I should trust him more.

"Hey, what did you think of that girl with the chainsaw?"

I look up. Sandy's talking about that girl from the training course. I knew she was his type. He was putting on a bit of an extra show for her.

"Nice."

"Nice?" Sandy bursts out laughing. "Did you see the tits on her?"

"Yeah, sure."

Sandy's eyes narrow. "You like someone else, don't you?"

I feel my cheeks explode. "No, no way."

Sandy laughs. "Yeah, you do. Who is it?"

"No one."

"Do I have to use my knife?"

"Whatever," I say.

It's quiet for a moment, but then Sandy says, "Is it . . . a neighbor?"

When I don't react, he whistles. "Nell? You kidding me? It's Nell."

There's no point denying it. Sandy always sees through me, even with three layers of makeup on my face.

"You got good taste," says Sandy. "But it's not very . . . practical."

Of course it's not practical. I know that myself. But from the very first moment I saw Nell, I knew I'd never be able to get her out of my mind. When she's around, I become aware of every fiber in my body. I can't explain it to Sandy. I don't think he's ever felt that way about a girl.

At that moment, the music stops. Sandy and I both look over our shoulders and hear a man's voice through a loud-speaker, welcoming the Fright Nighters.

When the man finishes, everyone cheers. The ground under our feet feels like it's shaking.

It's finally here. Fright Night has begun.

MURDERER

All those Fright Nighters together,
the tension in the air . . .
You could feel that something special was about to happen.
And we were there.
Is that what you were thinking too?

I think you were looking forward to that night
as much as me.
You had no way of knowing it would be your last.

FRIGHT NIGHT

SOFIA

Quin curses under his breath. "It's so dark."

"Yeah, it's a Fright Night, not a Fright Morning," says Martin. He switches on the flashlight. "Which way do we go?"

"Follow the arrows," says Dylan.

He points and I see a luminous arrow hanging on a tree nearby. It's begun. There's no way back. When I handed in the contract, I felt my stomach twitch with suspense.

The farther we walk from the entrance, the darker the woods become. In the distance, I can already hear girls screaming. That's the group that left before us. We are the sixth group to set off, so luckily we don't have long to wait.

"I can't wait for the first Scare Zone," says Quin.

I have no idea what the zones are going to be like. Could Martin's story about the twelve hundred crickets really be true? I think about the reviews I read. There were even some posts from people saying, "Don't do it!" One of them said there's always someone who passes out.

I walk a bit closer behind Martin as we follow the direction of the first arrow. The first big scare could come at any moment. . . .

"I think there's someone standing over there," Nell says, pointing into the distance. My heart rate immediately sky-rockets. There are dozens of actors hidden in these woods, and the flashlight is pretty weak. Martin laughs.

"I certainly hope there's someone standing over there. That's what we paid for, isn't it?"

Fright Night wasn't cheap. I've already burned through my savings for the summer. The rest of this break I'll have to rely on the generosity of my parents and my friends.

We pass a wall. I bet there's someone behind it.

But nothing happens. The only sound is our own breathing.

"What is this? Fright Night for under-twelves?" begins Martin, but right at that moment someone jumps out from behind a tree on the other side of the path. He's holding a flashlight under his blood-covered face, and his eyes are manic.

"Girrrlie . . ." He reaches toward me, and I shriek and back away. "Are you here to see me?" He licks his lips. "Then come a little closer."

I feel a hand on my arm, pulling me away from the man. I don't see whose hand it is until we're out of the guy's reach. Dylan looks at me with a smile.

"You okay?"

I nod but I feel my heart pounding against my ribs. Why am I being such a drama queen? I knew something like that was going to happen, didn't I?

"What a creep." Nell shivers. "That blood . . . He nearly grabbed your jacket!"

I don't like the thought of actors touching you. If we're not allowed to touch them, why are they allowed to touch us?

A few yards away, a flashlight suddenly goes on. I see a thin man standing on the path. He has bags under his eyes and a chalk-white face. It's like a scene from a horror movie.

"Good evening."

His voice is deep and ominous. His gray hair is tied back in a ponytail, and he's wearing an immaculate three-piece suit.

"Great. Another creep," Nell whispers.

"Why's he standing so still?" I whisper back. I know he's going to pounce just when we're least expecting it.

"Come closer. There's no need to be afraid of me."

No need to be afraid? This is Fright Night! But the five of us obediently shuffle forward.

"Which one of you is"—the man looks around our group—"Quin?"

A deathly silence falls. How does he know our names?

But then I remember my list of fears. They know exactly who all the Fright Nighters are. There's a reason why the organizers leave a little time between groups. It's so the actors know exactly which groups are coming and what their greatest fears are.

"I'm Quin," I hear beside me. When I look at him, I can't see a trace of fear on his face. How can he stay so calm?

"Are you ready?" The man beckons with his white-gloved hand.

Quin frowns. "Ready for what exactly, sir?"

The man smiles. "Ready for your death."

DYLAN

The actor takes us deeper into the trees.

Since when is Quin scared of dying? He's never said anything about it to me. Maybe he just wrote that down because he couldn't think of anything else. Death is a logical answer, though. It must be among the top three fears.

But it's not one of mine.

"No!" My eyes fill with tears. "I don't want to!"

The tunnel I have to go into for the brain scan is way too small. How will I ever be able to breathe in there?

"The doctor just needs to look inside your head." Mom grabs my wrists so I can't move. "Just calm down!"

I thrash my legs around.

"Mrs. Dumont." Dr. Savory places a hand on Mom's shoulder. "Why don't you go wait in the corridor?"

Mom never lets anyone send her away. She's always there, somewhere in the shadows. But to my surprise she goes.

Dr. Savory comes and sits on the edge of the bed. "Why are you so frightened?"

I look at the corridor, where I can see Mom through the glass. She's pacing back and forth.

"Are you afraid of the tunnel?"

I nod.

"It's really quick, honestly. It'll be over before you know it. Do you want to listen to some music?"

I look up. "Can I?"

"Sure." There's that sparkle in her eyes again.

"Thank you, Doctor," I say quietly. I'd behaved badly. Mom's going to be mad at me later.

"Just call me Eliza." Dr. Savory gives me a wink. "Because that's my name."

"We're here." The man stops in front of a small concrete building.

Martin curiously runs his flashlight over the windows, but they have garbage bags taped over them to block out the light.

"You're expected." The man bows and walks back in the direction we came from.

I'm suddenly delighted I'm not in Quin's shoes, but he doesn't seem at all bothered.

"Here goes." Quin pushes the door open.

We step into a small room with speakers on the ceiling, four chairs, and a low coffee table with magazines on it. The most remarkable thing about the room is the one-way mirror, the kind they have in police stations so they can keep an eye on the suspect. There's nothing to see, just our own reflections.

As Martin turns off the flashlight, the door beside the window opens. This man looks even creepier than his friend. He's wearing white face paint and red contacts, so it looks like his eyes are bleeding. It's a gruesome sight, but I can't stop looking.

"Quin Larkin?"

Quin raises his hand without hesitation.

"This way, please."

What's going to happen? Before I can ask, the door closes behind them. I hear a key being turned on the other side.

It's suddenly deathly silent in the room.

Sofia is the first to speak. "What on earth is this?"

"I don't know. I can't see anything." Nell peers through the glass, but the room behind is pitch dark. The fluorescent tube on the ceiling flickers.

"This is horrible," Sofia says quietly.

"It's supposed to be horrible." Martin tries to look through the glass too. "The tickets were way too expensive for just a few horror effects in the woods. Fright Night goes way beyond that. They really do go to extremes."

Quin told us this afternoon that the safe word was used seventeen times by last year's Fright Nighters, an all-time record. He said he hoped the record would be broken this year.

Loud organ music blasts out of the speakers. Nell and Martin jump back as the room behind the glass slowly lights up. The man is standing between two big candleholders. I see a platform with a purple-lined wooden casket on it.

And inside that casket lies Quin. His hands are crossed on his chest, and his eyes are closed.

I feel my blood racing through my body. Is this real? No, it can't be. And yet . . . it looks so real, like Quin has actually been laid to rest.

"Welcome, dearly beloved." I don't take in another word of the man's speech. All my attention is on Quin, lying there motionless in the casket.

What if he really died? I'd never be able to laugh with him again. He'd never be able to irritate me again with his comments about Sofia. I'd never be woken up by his snoring.

Maybe Hester and Johan would send me away, because they couldn't handle it. Then where would I go? I'd probably end up in some kind of institution, most likely in another town. And then I'd lose Sofia too. I feel my panic mounting.

The man picks up the casket lid, which is leaning against the wall. It slowly dawns on me what's going to happen. I pound my fists against the glass, as if I can get through it.

"This has to be a joke," I hear Martin say.

The man fastens the lid to the casket with six screws. With each screw, I press my hands harder against the glass. This has to stop!

"I can't watch this." Nell turns her face away.

Then he opens a metal hatch in the wall. There's a bright light, which I immediately recognize as fire.

"No . . ."

I glance at Sofia. Her eyes are so wide it seems like they might pop out of their sockets at any moment.

"He's going to cremate Quin!"

KELLY

"So . . . Nell."

Sandy gives me a sideways look. We walk deeper into the woods, away from our place behind the wall. According to Sandy, the Insect Zone is where we need to be.

"Doesn't she have a boyfriend?"

I shake my head. "No."

Sandy sniffs. "Nell is a neighbor."

I sigh.

"Have you been . . . flirting with her?"

"A bit."

"But you're too chicken to take it any further, huh?"

I hate that Sandy knows me so well. When we go to clubs, he's always the one who goes over and talks to the cool girls, and I usually end up with their boring friends.

"I'm going to ask her out tomorrow."

Sandy grimaces. "Is that such a good idea?"

"Why?"

"She's a neighbor," Sandy says again. "If she rejects you, you'll have to see her every day."

I know he's right, but I don't want to hear it.

"She won't reject me," I say.

"How can you be so certain?"

I think about the way Nell bit her lip. She sat so close to me on Monday that I could smell her perfume. She started talking about a wedding ring and she looked at me in the way only she can.

"I just know."

"I give up on you."

"Whatever."

I don't want to talk about Nell anymore. Sandy doesn't get it anyway. He thinks Nell is the same as all the other neighbors, but she's different with me. She lets me come close. She tells me personal stuff. You don't do that with just anyone, do you?

"Hey, why are we going this way?" I look around. "This route is a complete detour!"

"We're making a little stop on the way."

"What kind of stop?"

Sandy grins. "A chainsaw stop."

I should have known. Even on Fright Night, Sandy is still chasing after girls. "Do we have to do this now?"

"Sure we do." Sandy reaches into his pocket. For a moment, I think he's going to grab the knife again, but then he brings out a cigarette.

"You can't smoke here."

"Chill a bit. You're so stressed." Sandy takes out another cigarette. "Here, you could do with one."

"I quit."

"Oh yeah. Remind me why."

"It's a pact with Nell."

Sandy rolls his eyes. "That girl is messing with your head, Kelly."

SOFIA

The organ music swells as Quin's casket is pushed into the oven.

"Quin!" Like Dylan, I bang on the glass, but there's absolutely no point. All that happens is the music stops and the light behind the glass goes off. The only thing I can see is my own reflection. A pale face with big, anxious eyes.

Martin laughs. "Calm down. Do you really think they're going to burn your friend alive?"

I know he's right, but I can't be that rational right now. This is about Quin, not some stranger. Martin would go crazy if Nell was in there too!

"Now we've just got to wait for Quin to come back." Martin sits on one of the chairs. I feel too jittery to sit down, but at the same time my legs are like lead. If this is just the beginning of Fright Night, what else do they have in store for us?

"Quin's okay," Nell reassures me as she comes to sit beside me. "Or he'd have used the safe word."

She's right. There's always a way out. If we shout "Ketchup!" the actors have to stop what they're doing. Quin could have used the word if he was really in danger.

"It was terrifying to watch, but it wasn't real." The comforting tone of Nell's voice calms me down. Suddenly I feel ashamed for losing it like that. She must think I'm . . .

"Sorry," I say quietly.

"No problem. It's not every day you see your friend supposedly die."

The way it comes out is so dry that all four of us burst out laughing.

Nell sighs and leans back. "What a night. And it's only just started."

I nod and look at my watch. How long will it be before Quin comes back?

Nell twists the ring on her index finger. I notice she has one on every finger, except for her actual ring finger.

"Are you saving that one for your wedding ring?"

Nell smiles. "Exactly."

I take a quick look at Martin. Are the two of them a couple? I think they kind of go together.

"Maybe," says Nell when she sees me looking. She whispers, "Martin's a pretty good candidate."

Then she looks at Dylan. "And what about you?"

I rub the beads on my wrist. "Just good friends," I say quietly.

"You never know. Things can turn out strangely. Where I work, things go differently from I expect every day."

Martin looks up. "Is this about that Kelvin guy?"

"You know very well that's not what he goes by," says Nell.

Martin sniffs. "I don't get why you hang out with that lunatic."

"It's my job to spend time with him."

"Not like you do. You need to keep a bit of distance. You can't trust those guys."

Nell clenches her jaw and doesn't reply. What is this about?

"What kind of work do you do?" I ask curiously.

Nell's angry expression disappears. "I'm a student, but I do volunteer work too. I'm what they call a *neighbor*. It means I live by a special housing complex where young people without a safe home environment get the chance to learn to live independently."

"That sounds cool."

"It is. What about you? Hey, who are you anyway?"

I burst out laughing. She's right—we haven't had much time to get to know each other at all. Before we'd even introduced ourselves properly, Fright Night had already started.

"I'm still in high school. We moved here at the beginning of this year, and I ended up in Dylan and Quin's class."

When he hears his name, Dylan looks up.

"What about you?" Nell asks.

Dylan fidgets on his chair. "What do you want to know?"

Nell smiles. "Whatever you want to tell me."

I remember what Gerda said. Dylan had spent weeks in bed, but what was wrong with him? Was he being treated for something?

"You got some kind of injury?" I hear Nell ask. She's pointing at Dylan's right leg, which he's resting on the coffee table.

"No. It's been like that for ages. A broken bone that never really healed."

"Ouch. How did it happened?"

Dylan shrugs. "A hockey stick whacked my shinbone in elementary school."

"Nasty."

It takes a second to sink in, but then my gaze shoots to Dylan. A hockey stick? He told me he fell off his bike! I can remember the moment well. We were at the pool and I asked him about it. So why is he giving a completely different answer now?

At that moment, the door swings open. My body instantly leaps back into Fright Night mode. But then I see that it's Quin. He's grinning from ear to ear, and he looks far from dead.

"So, who missed me?"

DYLAN

We walk back outside, Martin leading the way with the flashlight.

"I don't get you," Sofia says to Quin. "That went way too far."

"Too far? What do you mean?"

"You were burned alive! Or . . . we thought you were!"

"I know." Quin grins. "It got really hot inside that casket. I think they must have used a heater."

"It's sick," says Sofia. She's not wrong. Even if you know it's fake, it's horrible to see your best friend laid out inside a casket like that. And to watch it burn.

I touch the arms of my glasses. I push them down a bit, so they bite deeper into the skin behind my ears.

"They're on straight," I hear Sofia say. She's come to walk beside me. Quin's gone to join Martin, who's as enthusiastic about his death as Quin is himself.

"Your glasses," says Sofia. "They're on straight. They're always on straight."

I feel my cheeks getting warm. She's been watching me.

"Sorry, it's a tic."

"I know. I have one too. With my bracelet." She turns my gift around her wrist. "I touch the beads to calm myself down."

"And does it help?"

Sofia smiles. "Maybe not tonight."

"We'll survive," I say with a grin.

Sofia points at my glasses. "How strong are the lenses?"

My cheeks flush again. I'm glad Sofia doesn't have the flashlight in her hands because then she'd be sure to notice.

"I'm just about blind without them," I say. If she knew why I first started wearing them . . .

Mom looks at me from behind the steering wheel. "Why didn't you say you're having trouble with your eyes?"

I squeeze my eyes shut to block out the bright sunshine. "It's just the light."

"You see! I knew it." Mom sits up straighter. "I've read about this. It all confirms it."

"Confirms what, Mom?"

"Multiple sclerosis."

They are difficult words. I try to repeat them, but I can't. I just stumble over the syllables.

"Multiple sclerosis," Mom says again. "It's just as well your mom pays such close attention, because it can be fatal."

Fatal? What is Mom saying?

Mom turns the car into the hospital parking lot. "When we see Dr. Savory, you have to tell her you're having problems with your eyes."

I'm still walking next to Sofia. Whenever actors jump out of the darkness, she automatically grabs my arm. Her fingers must be leaving bruises, but I don't care. I like doing this with her. It feels like we're a team within our group, just the two of us.

"Sorry," says Sofia, grabbing my arm yet again.

"It's okay." I rub the spot she just squeezed, which is starting to feel kind of tender. "I'm more attached to my left arm anyway."

Sofia laughs. "Hey, what's the story with your leg? You told me you'd fallen off your bike, but just now you said to Nell it was a hockey stick."

She says it so casually that it takes me a couple of seconds to grasp exactly what she's saying.

"Did I?" My mouth suddenly feels dry. This conversation just went 180 degrees. I really need to be careful now.

"At the pool," Sofia reminds me. "When I asked you about it."

I forgot about that. How can I have been so dumb? Quin knows only half the story, but I completely lied to Sofia. Why, though? Was I scared she'd see through me if I told her just half of the truth?

Suddenly there's a weird roaring sound beside us. Someone

jumps out from behind a tree holding a huge chainsaw. The noise is deafening. The look in the actress's eyes is dark and sinister.

"You need to keep looking!"

Eliza shakes her head. "We have looked, Mrs. Dumont. Your son is—"

"But I think he has MS! He has all the symptoms, from muscle weakness to dizziness. He's not sleeping well, and now his eyes are giving him trouble."

Eliza looks at me. "Is that right, Dylan?"

Mom's eyes speak a language I understand better than anyone.

"Maybe he just needs glasses," Eliza says to Mom. "Did you think of that?"

"Run!" I hear someone yell.

The flashing teeth of the chainsaw come closer and closer.

"Dylan!"

Why won't my legs work?

"That woman acts like I'm crazy!" Mom's driving way too fast through the traffic.

"Maybe Eliza's right, Mom. I don't feel sick."

Suddenly Mom brakes. She pulls halfway off the road, onto the shoulder. A car tears past, its horn beeping.

*Mom lashes out. The palm of her hand meets my cheek, and
her voice crackles like fireworks.*

"Do. Not. Lie!"

The teeth of the chainsaw are only a few inches away now. The
actress yells something at me, but it doesn't sink in.

"Dylan!"

I feel a hand around my wrist and almost stumble over my
own feet as I'm dragged away from the chainsaw and away
from those dark eyes. Then there's a hard punch on my shoulder, which brings me straight back to Fright Night.

"You idiot! Why did you just stand there?" Quin glares at
me furiously. "You almost got that chainsaw in your face!"

It feels like my head is full of cotton balls. What exactly did
I do wrong?

"You are totally Mr. Fright." Quin swears and shakes his
head. "If Sofia hadn't dragged you away, we really would need
a casket right now."

I look back, but the actress with the chainsaw is nowhere
to be seen. What happened to me? Why couldn't I run away,
like anyone else would? It was almost like it was Mom looking
at me.

Am I going crazy? I can feel the whole group staring at me.
This isn't smart. The last thing I want to do is draw attention
to myself.

"I was just startled," I say quickly. "It won't happen again."

KELLY

"And a very good evening to you."

The girl with the chainsaw turns around. As soon as she sees us, she lowers the saw.

"What are you guys doing here?"

Sandy shrugs. "Thought we'd come by and say hi. How's it going?"

"You just missed the weirdest thing. I went after this guy with my saw—and he just stood there!"

"Maybe he wanted to die," says Sandy solemnly.

"Seemed more like he was in shock or something."

Sandy holds out his hand to shake hers. "I'm Sandy and this is Kelly."

"Melody."

Sandy doesn't let go of her hand. "Melody . . . Nice name."

I sigh audibly.

"Ignore him. Kelly's just in a bad mood." Sandy puts his arm around me. "Maybe you have a nice friend who could cheer him up?"

I shake off Sandy's arm. What's he up to now?

"A friend? What do you mean?"

"Like a double date. You and me, and Kelly and your friend."

"Hey, there's no need," I say quickly. Hasn't Sandy been paying attention? There's only one girl I want to date, and I'm going to ask her tomorrow morning.

"Yes, there is." Sandy leans over to Melody and says, just loud enough for me to hear: "He has a broken heart."

I clench my jaw. What I really want to do is kick Sandy but then, to add insult to injury, Melody nods.

"I'm sure it'll work out."

"Nice." Sandy gives her a wink. "Tomorrow?"

"Cool." Melody raises her chainsaw. "I have to get back to work."

"Us too," says Sandy. "Do you know the quickest route to the Insect Zone?"

...

"What do you think you're doing?!" I shout as soon as we're out of earshot. We're walking straight through the woods.

"Looking for a better spot, like I said."

"I mean with Melody!" My voice rises. "I don't have a broken heart!"

"Not yet."

"And what's that supposed to mean?"

"That it's never going to work between Nell and you."

"Because she's a neighbor?"

"Exactly." Sandy stops and puts his hands on my shoulders. I can hardly look into his yellow eyes. It's like I'm being hypnotized.

"I'm doing this for you, Kelly. I just don't want that girl to hurt you."

"She won't."

"All the neighbors are the same. They're there to help us and to keep an eye on us. They're above us."

"Nell's not like that. You weren't there on Monday. She was totally flirting with me!"

"How?"

I don't want to tell him, but I have to. Sandy needs to understand that Nell's different.

"She bit her bottom lip, she laughed at my jokes, she—"

"Then you should have kissed her," Sandy says, interrupting me. "That way you'd have known for certain."

"Don't be dumb."

"It's what you want, isn't it?"

"Of course, but—"

"So when are you going to do it? When you're forty? You saw how smoothly it went with Melody just now."

"I'm not you."

"We're more alike than you think."

"No, we are not. And it's you who's causing problems here!"

Sandy sighs. "Problems are what we're made of, Kelly. Get that into your skull."

"Nell doesn't see it like that. She thinks I'm normal, even after I told her about the past."

Sandy's eyebrows shoot up. "Did you tell her about . . ."

I nod. "I said I destroyed someone's life because of hate."

Sandy shakes his head. "You know it's the other way around too."

"Says you."

"It's what you should be saying as well. You did what you did for a reason."

I know Sandy and I aren't going to agree about this, but at the same time it feels good that he always defends me. As he has since day one.

"Anyway, Nell said we've all done stuff we're not proud of. She actually reacted really well."

Sandy gives me a skeptical look. "So she didn't run away screaming?"

"Nope," I say. "Do you see that Nell's different now?"

Then Sandy's face clouds over. He's looking at a point behind me.

"What's wrong?"

When I turn around, I see a group of people walking among the trees. Right at the back, I see someone I recognize even by the glow of a single flashlight.

I feel my eyes widening. "Nell . . ."

SOFIA

Dylan just stood there. While that crazy girl waved the chain-saw around, he just stood there. Luckily, I was able to pull him away in time, or otherwise the teeth of the chainsaw could have hit him.

I look at Dylan as he follows Quin and Martin. He's hardly said another word since the chainsaw. What was going on in-side his head? It seemed like he was in shock. I see that he's dragging his right leg. Looks like he's in pain.

"Let's take a break," I call over to them.

Martin turns around in surprise. "What? Now?"

"Just a quick one." I drop down beside Nell, but I can't take my eyes off Dylan. He's just staring ahead, while Quin and Martin are talking about the next zone.

What's wrong with him?

"Are you worried?" asks Nell.

I look up. "A bit."

"What happened?"

"He stood there. He was completely out of it, and he didn't even react to his own name."

"I think he's kind of special."

Strangely, the way Nell says it doesn't sound like an insult at all.

"Yeah, he is. Dylan's a pretty private person. He doesn't like talking about himself and sometimes I have no idea where I stand with him." I'm shocked by my own words. It feels like I'm betraying Dylan. "I don't mean that in a bad way," I say quickly.

Nell smiles. "I know."

"Some things just aren't . . . right, though." I fiddle with my bracelet. "He tells lies."

"What about?"

When I hesitate, Nell puts her hand on my arm. "I'll keep my mouth shut."

"His leg," I say. "He told you it was a hockey stick, but he told me a completely different story. When I just confronted him about it, he got really twitchy."

Nell nods. "I know those kinds of lies. Sometimes they forget what they've said themselves."

"*They?*"

Nell smiles. "The kids at the housing complex where I live."

I look at Dylan again, who's still staring at the ground in front of him. It's maybe a bit of an exaggeration to compare him to those problem kids, but there's definitely something going on with him. Something he doesn't show to me, maybe not even to Quin.

. . .

88

We have to keep going, or the next group will catch up with us. Dylan is walking beside me again, but he's still not saying anything.

The relaxed atmosphere between us has pretty much evaporated. I want to talk to him, but how do I start?

Hey, Dylan, I was just wondering. Have you ever been really, really sick?

I put my hands in the pockets of my denim jacket. Through the fabric, I can feel something jabbing into my skin. The photo and postcard from Dylan's old house are still in there. The words on the card go through my head again.

One day I'm going to kill you.

Maybe the postcard was meant for him. Maybe there's a whole world around Dylan that I know nothing about.

I shake off that idea. It makes no sense. Everyone has secrets, don't they? It's not a crime for Dylan not to tell me everything.

"What's the matter?"

Dylan looks at me expectantly, and I realize he must be talking to me.

"With me? Nothing. Why?" My voice squeaks a bit. You see, we all lie.

"You look worried." Dylan's expression is guilty now. "Sorry if I gave you a fright."

"It's okay. I get that you were just shocked."

Maybe I should let it go. What if I drive him away again with my questions? I decide to change the subject.

"You going to see your mom tomorrow?"

Dylan looks at me in surprise. "Of course."

"So where do you actually go when you visit her?"

"You know, just back home."

It's like he fired a bullet at me. Home? Gerda said she's been looking after the house while Dylan's mom is away! Dylan doesn't know that I know, but now I'm sure he's been lying about other things too.

And the way he does it, so easily—that hurts.

"What about your dad?" Quin told me Dylan doesn't have any contact with his dad. But I've never dared ask about it before.

I can barely hear the answer, but Dylan says, "My dad was a douche."

I look at him. Dylan's eyes are glinting in a way I've never seen before.

"What do you mean?"

"Fathers are supposed to take care of their kids. Well, he didn't. I never knew him."

I can hear the tension in his voice. This time Dylan's not lying. I'm certain of that.

"And your mom? Do you miss her?"

"Children should be with their mothers, shouldn't they?"

I nod. "So . . . what's wrong with her?"

"Cancer."

The word sounds so harsh coming out of his mouth. It's like a curse. Such a serious sickness—is that what Dylan had too? The thought of him spending all that time at home in bed—it hits me hard. He shouldn't be carrying something like that all by himself. He should be able to talk about it. He can trust me.

90

"I'd like to go with you tomorrow," I say.

Dylan stops in his tracks. "Why?"

He sounds almost defensive.

"I . . . I'd like to meet her."

That's not so weird, is it? Dylan comes to my place all the time.

"That . . . that's not going to work. She's sick." Dylan reaches for his glasses. That tic he has when he's nervous.

"Another time, then?" I suggest.

"Yeah . . . yeah, sure." Dylan speeds up and goes to walk with Quin. He clearly can't get away from me quickly enough. He's running away from me.

I don't get it. Dylan's answers seem so random, like they're about someone else, not him.

Sometimes they forget what they've said themselves.

I thought Nell was exaggerating before, but now I'm not so sure.

Dylan laughs out loud at something Quin says. He can switch, just like that. Why have I never noticed that before? I think he's hiding so much that he's lost track. That's why he gives such strange answers that don't match up.

What does this mean? Something is going on with him. I'm sure of it. My gut feeling doesn't lie.

Dylan could well be wearing the best mask this Fright Night.

MURDERER

Insect Zone.
A shiver ran down my spine when I saw those words.
Did you feel the same?

Looking back, I'm not so sure.
Maybe the shiver wasn't because of the words at all,
but because I felt something was going to happen.
I think your death was already hanging in the air at
that point.

DYLAN

Why did Sofia suddenly start talking about my family? She even wants to go see Mom.

Another time, then, she suggested, but there's no way that can happen. I really need to be more careful with the answers I give. I'm getting sloppy. She's already realized I've been telling different stories about my leg, and she could soon discover a lot more.

"I have something for you." Mom comes into my room with a case in her hand. She takes out a pair of glasses with round frames. It was an old pair of hers. She's been wearing lenses for years.

"F-for me?" I stammer. When Eliza had mentioned glasses, Mom got mad. So why is she giving me glasses now? Mom puts the glasses in my hands. "Give them a try?"

Reluctantly, I put them on. My room becomes blurry.

"Excellent," I hear Mom say. "From now on, you can wear them every day."

"We're here." Quin grins. He points at a board above our heads with the words INSECT ZONE written on it in curly letters.

The second zone of the night. All that stuff with the chainsaw and the conversation with Sofia has tired me out. All I really want to do is turn around and go back to the entrance, but then a woman suddenly looms out of the darkness. She's wearing an apron covered in nasty stains and she has a chef's hat on her head. In her hands is a plastic box with a lid on it.

"Twelve hundred crickets wouldn't fit in there," I hear Quin joke.

I glance at Sofia, who's clinging to Nell. The two of them are standing as far away from the woman as they can.

What's the likelihood they both put insects as one of their fears? Now I can't leave. I have to help Sofia, like she just helped me. It's not her fault I have so many secrets to remember.

"Did someone say something?" The woman looks at us, one by one. When no one reacts, she gives a satisfied nod. "Because when I'm speaking, you guys keep quiet. Got it?"

Quin chuckles quietly. "Is she always this bad?"

"Shut your mouth! You might think this is all a fun night out, but it isn't. You're in the chef's kitchen now—and you're going to regret ever signing up for Fright Night."

We all fall silent. Strangely, I forget that we're dealing with an actress. This woman really seems angry.

I look at the box in her hands. What could be in there?

"My name's Marouska." The chef looks at us. "And which of you is . . . Sofia?"

I curse to myself. If what the reviews say is true, and it gets worse from zone to zone, then Sofia is in for something pretty nasty.

Sofia doesn't respond.

"Sofia?" repeats Marouska.

Still no reaction. I see Quin give her a nudge, but Sofia still refuses to step forward. Does she think she's going to get away with it that easily?

"I cooked something specially for you." Marouska takes off the lid and I hear little legs scratching away inside the box. What's in there?

I stand on tiptoe, but then I hear Nell's voice behind me. "Cockroaches."

Marouska looks at Nell and Sofia. "One of you is Sofia. And you aren't going anywhere until you've tasted my special entrée."

Tasted? She's got to be kidding. I once watched this TV show where the participants had to eat live insects, but never cockroaches. Just the thought of it makes me want to puke.

As Marouska lowers the box, I see dozens of cockroaches climbing over each other. She's getting impatient. When there's still no reaction from Sofia, she threateningly takes out her walkie-talkie.

"Do you want to quit?" She presses a button.

"Hello?" says a voice at the other end.

"I have group number six here. They're quitting."

I see Quin signaling to Sofia. He doesn't want to stop. Fright Night's not even halfway through.

"Come on," says Martin quietly. "These tickets were so expensive."

What a dumb thing to say! I'm about to stick up for Sofia, but then she steps forward.

"Okay. I'm Sofia."

Marouska puts the walkie-talkie to her mouth. "False alarm."

She puts away the walkie-talkie and looks at Sofia, all smiles now. "Good. I hope you're hungry."

The cockroaches in the box are getting twitchier, like they sense what's about to happen.

I can't watch this. Sofia's terrified—she has been since the beginning of Fright Night. Does she really have to do this?

Sofia takes off her jacket. Her hands get stuck in the sleeves and she frantically shakes it off. Then she slowly moves her hand toward the box. Her fingers are shaking.

It feels like I'm watching myself as I wait for the next shot, the next test, the next doctor. Sofia's going to have nightmares about this for months. She's going to wake up in a cold sweat, just like me, over and over again.

I can't let that happen to her, can I?

"Why aren't you wearing your glasses?" Mom is already sitting at the breakfast table when I come downstairs.

I'd deliberately left the glasses on my bedside table. The strength of the lenses gave me a thumping headache.

"Don't lie to me," Mom says. "You know I hate liars."

"I forgot them," I say.

Mom slaps me again. It's like her hand has left a permanent impression.

"Go get your glasses. Now."

On an impulse, I lean forward and reach into the box.

Then, without thinking about it, I stuff the cockroach into my mouth.

SOFIA

"No!" But my voice is lost in the moment.

"Don't forget to chew," I hear Marouska say.

There's a cracking sound. The cockroach's shell breaks between Dylan's teeth.

What's he doing? This was *my* fear, not his.

Dylan chews almost rhythmically with his eyes closed, and then swallows the bug. The Insect Zone is completely silent. Even Marouska isn't saying anything. Then Dylan opens his eyes and looks at me. We stare at each other for a couple of seconds and I see his cheeks flush. He did that for me.

"Um, g-great . . . awesome," stammers Marouska, who seems to have forgotten the part she's playing. "I guess you can, um, continue."

...

"You are brilliant. And crazy." Quin slaps Dylan on the shoulder, with a big grin on his face. "What did it taste like? Like a big old booger?"

98

Dylan shakes his head. "Kind of nutty. But with legs."

Martin shudders. "You have gone insane. You just ate a live cockroach, man!"

"Yup. I know."

I want to thank Dylan, but how can I ever thank him enough? It feels like he just saved my life by taking on my task. What if I'd had to eat that cockroach? How could I have done it? I'd never have dared, no matter how hard Martin was pushing because of the expensive tickets. Eating a live cockroach is going way too far. Those little legs tickling your tongue . . . I shiver. I bet loads of groups get stuck at this stage.

Nell nudges me. "Where's your jacket?"

I realize I'm walking around with bare arms. "Oh no, what an idiot. I forgot it."

"What's up?" Quin looks back.

"Sofia forgot her jacket."

"I'll go fetch it." Dylan takes the flashlight from Martin and jogs off. It's like the cockroach gave him new energy.

"Back soon," he calls.

DYLAN

I did it. I just went and did it.

The cockroach didn't taste nutty. It was gross. But I did it for her. The way Sofia looked at me when I'd swallowed the cockroach made it all worthwhile. She looked at me like I was her hero.

I head back to the Insect Zone as quickly as I can. Our flashlight is acting up. I slap it a few times, but it keeps flickering.

"You again?" Marouska smiles. "You want another one?"

"No, thank you." I make straight for Sofia's jacket, which is bundled up on the ground nearby. I pick it up and walk away.

Halfway back, I pause and look around. No one can see me, so I lift the jacket to my face. I breathe in Sofia's familiar scent. She feels close and yet so very far away. If I want to be honest with her, I have to be honest about everything. Then I have to tell her about the past.

Can I do that?

I want to try at least. I don't want to push her away from

me. I want to bring her closer. I want her to look at me the way she did just now. Every single day.

As I lower the jacket, I spot something sticking out of her inside pocket.

Curiously, I pull it out and see that it's a postcard. The picture on the front almost takes my breath away.

Stunned, I stare at the big blue lake with the trees around it, the lake that made such an impression on me I could draw it with my eyes closed. I wished the summer vacation we spent there could have gone on forever. We swam, built forts, and ate as much ice cream as we could shovel down. We were happy, for the first time and the last.

How did Sofia get this postcard? Did someone she know go there on vacation?

But then I see something lying on the ground. It must have fallen from Sofia's pocket when I pulled out the card.

I bend to pick it up, but I freeze halfway.

It's a photograph—with two faces staring up at me.

Even in the flicker of the flashlight, I recognize them immediately, but I can't see how they fit.

Not here, not on Fright Night.

And definitely not inside Sofia's pocket.

SOFIA

Why's Dylan taking so long? Just as I'm about to go look for him, I see a flickering beam of light. Dylan's coming back with my denim jacket. Just as I'm about to take it from him, I see what he has in his other hand.

The photograph of him and his mom.

"Where did you get this?" Dylan's voice sounds different. Deep, distant, miles away. For a moment, I forget to answer.

"What is it?" Quin looks at his friend. "What did you find?"

"I asked you a question." Dylan's staring at me. "Where did you get this?"

Why's he so mad about it? I feel myself automatically taking a step back.

Dylan's eyes narrow. "And did you go into my room?"

He knows . . . My cheeks flush.

"What the hell are you doing?!" yells Dylan. He's firing all these questions at me, but barely giving me time to answer.

Quin's eyebrows rise. "No, what are *you* doing? Calm down, man."

"I *am* calm." Dylan's voice trembles. "I want to know why Sofia's doing . . . research into me."

Research? This is going all wrong.

"It's for your birthday," I say quickly.

But Dylan's not listening. The words are pouring from his mouth like lava.

"You're researching me! That's why you were asking all those questions about the past. That's why you wanted to know all about my dad. That's why you want to come see Mom tomorrow. And I thought it was because . . . because . . ."

What's he talking about? I'm desperately searching for the right words, but Quin beats me to it.

"Why would Sofia be doing *research* into you?"

Dylan holds up the photograph. "So she's just carrying this around for no reason?"

Quin tilts his head to look at the picture. "Hey, that's—"

"I know who it is!" Dylan points at me. "I just want to know why *she* is walking around with it!"

"She just told you, didn't she? It's for your birthday."

"Keep out of it, Quin!" I've never heard Dylan yell, certainly not at his best friend. And judging by the shocked look on Quin's face, it's the first time for him too.

"What?"

"This isn't about you. This is about *her*!"

It feels like I'm slowly disappearing into a whirlpool. I'm spinning around and around, and I can't get out. What is happening here?

Quin grabs Dylan by the arms. "Calm down, idiot."

DYLAN

"Let go of me!"

Quin's hands are like two vises around my arms. The people in the hospital sometimes held me like that when I needed another injection. Mom often helped them too. Her hands always left the most bruises.

I jerk away and my arms shoot free. My right hand smashes into the side of Quin's head.

Quin clutches his face and gapes at me. The silence that follows is deafening.

His eyes start to gleam and before I know what's happening, he takes a swing at me. As his fist hits my face, I hear something crack.

My head is thumping as if little men are kicking my skull from the inside. It won't take Mom long to notice my headache. And then she'll use it against me.

After school, I don't cycle home but go downtown to an optician's office.

"Do you sell these frames?" I put Mom's old glasses on the counter.

The assistant looks at the brand and shakes her head. I'm about to leave when she says, "But we do stock something similar."

I breathe a sigh of relief. It's going to be okay.

The woman picks up a pair of glasses that are just like Mom's.

"How much are they?"

"The frame's seventy, but if you add in the lenses—"

"I don't need prescription lenses," I say quickly. "The lenses that are in them will do fine."

The woman frowns. "But they're just plastic and—"

"That's okay."

I reach into the pocket of my jeans. It took all my savings, including the birthday money the neighbor had given me, but it's worth it.

"Here you go." I put my money on the counter and pick up the new pair of glasses. When I put them on, the world looks normal again.

I leave Mom's old glasses behind on the counter.

Something's really wrong. I can feel it. When I take off my glasses, I groan.

The frame's completely bent, and one of the arms is sticking out at a weird angle.

It slowly dawns on me. Quin bust my glasses. The glasses I bought to fool Mom.

I fought back. For once in my life, I fought back. And I

wear the proof on my face every day, but now that proof is broken.

"Sorry." Quin's words come from a long way off. "I didn't mean to . . ."

Tears blur my vision as I look up. Quin would never understand. If anything of his breaks, his mom and dad just buy him a new one. That's just what his parents do.

Blood rushes through my body and I dive forward. I catch Quin off guard, and we fall onto the ground. I feel a foot in my ribs and kick him wherever I can with my good leg.

"Hey!" shouts a loud voice. "Stop that! Now!"

Someone pulls me away. The fist that was meant for Quin hits thin air. I struggle and shout, but it doesn't help. Someone throws me up against a tree.

"You done?"

Now I see that it's Marouska. Martin's holding Quin by his T-shirt, and there's blood pouring from his nose.

"What's going on here?"

"Sorry," I hear Martin saying as he lets go of Quin. "They—"

"Were fighting," says Marouska, finishing his sentence for him. "I saw. And we don't tolerate any violence at Fright Night."

Martin nods. "I completely understand. But it's over now. Right, guys?"

It isn't over at all. This feels like it's just the beginning. How did Sophia get hold of that photo? There's only one and it's on our old windowsill, half hidden behind the curtain. She must have been inside the house, but how? And more important: why?

"I'm going to have to disqualify you." Marouska takes out her walkie-talkie again.

Martin shoots forward. "No, please don't. They're best friends. It was just a misunderstanding."

I look again at Quin's nose. The bleeding's getting worse.

"Hey, and Dylan did eat that cockroach, after all." Martin puts his hands together. "Please . . ."

Marouska looks at me, and her expression softens. "That's true. I've never seen anything like that before."

"Exactly." Martin seizes his chance. "It won't happen again. No more fighting. Promise."

Marouska narrows her eyes, as if trying to read me. There's a few seconds of silence. And then she says, "Go on, then. One last chance."

"Thanks. Thanks so much." Martin drags us along the path. As soon as we reach the next arrow, he explodes at us.

"What was all that about? You were like a couple of wild animals, the way you were rolling around! Quin, you're going to need to pinch your nose. Or you'll bleed out."

Quin leans against a tree and does as Martin says. It doesn't help much. The blood keeps coming.

Was it really me who did that to him? I look away, but then my eyes meet Sofia's. She's looking at me like I'm what Martin just described me as: a wild animal. And maybe it's true. My whole body's tingling. I'm like a volcano that's about to erupt.

I am lethal. I was right—this is just the beginning. When I explode, I'd better be as far as possible from Quin and Sofia, before I do damage that can't be repaired. I fold up the glasses with the bent arm and put them in my pocket.

"I'm leaving."

They all stare at me.

Martin shakes his head. "What? Where are you going?"

I shrug. "Away from here."

SOFIA

No one does anything. We just watch, stunned, as Dylan leaves.

Where is he going? Why did he explode like that?

I don't get it. This isn't the Dylan I know. The Dylan I know is patient and kind. He lets everyone push in front of him in line in the school cafeteria, he gives extra lunch money to freshmen, and he lends me and Quin his notes. So how can he suddenly change like that? When he hit Quin, it was like a scene in a movie.

I watch Dylan disappear into the darkness. He's dragging his right leg more than usual. Quin must have kicked it. How far does he think he's going to get without a flashlight? It's pitch dark, especially off the main path.

I have to go after him. I have to bring him back.

"No. You're staying here." Nell sees what I'm thinking. "I don't think it makes sense for the two of you to be around each other right now."

Nell's right—of course she is—but what I am supposed to do? This is all *my* fault. Dylan feels betrayed and I get that, but

I never meant to hurt him. I just wanted to make a nice gift for him. I want to help him. I should be able to explain that to him, shouldn't I?

"I'll go," says Quin. His face is a battlefield, and his T-shirt is covered in splashes of red.

"Is that such a great idea?" says Martin, looking at Quin's nose. "He might attack you again."

"It's Dylan," says Quin. "He won't do that."

"He didn't seem to have a problem with it just now."

"Something must be wrong. He doesn't usually act that strange."

Quin's right. That's definitely not the Dylan we know. Is it because he saw the photo? But why would that make him flip out? Or is it because I went into his room without asking? Was he scared I might find something there?

"Are you okay?"

A feeling of uneasiness comes over me when Quin looks at me with that worried expression. I don't deserve it. Okay, Dylan's reaction was over the top, but I was the one who tore our group apart.

I nod. "Be quick. And please bring him back."

KELLY

I can hear furious yelling and shouting somewhere nearby.

"What's that?" I feel my eyes widening. "Nell . . ."

"No, wait!" Sandy stops me. "You look like hell, you idiot. If you go over there now, she'll run away screaming."

I know he's right, but I have to make sure she's okay. As I shoot through the trees, the shouting dies down. I wait another couple of minutes and then creep the last few yards toward them.

"Are you okay?" I hear a boy ask.

"Be quick," a girl says. "And please bring him back."

I breathe a sigh of relief when I see Nell isn't there.

Someone walks away, and I quickly hide behind a big tree. Sandy squeezes himself in behind me, and I feel his breath on the back of my neck.

"Just give me a moment," says the same girl.

"Are you sure?" This time it's Nell. I'd recognize her voice anywhere.

"Certain."

"We're here if you need us." There's the sound of footsteps again. They stop a few yards in front of our tree.

"This isn't fun anymore, Martin," Nell says quietly. Before Sandy can stop me, I peer around the tree trunk. Nell's standing less than fifteen feet away, and she looks frightened. But she's still beautiful, maybe even more beautiful than ever. Fear suits her.

"It's all going to be okay," says the boy, who's tall and apparently called Martin. I've never seen him before. How do the two of them know each other?

"I think we should stop." Nell looks at him. "I have a bad feeling about this."

"Stop? But we've already come so far!" Martin puts his arm around her. All I want to do is jump out from behind the tree and knock him away from her, but instead I have to watch as Martin pulls Nell closer.

"Are you still mad?" I hear him asking. "You know I only get upset because I'm worried about you."

"There's no need. I can take care of myself just fine."

"I know that." Martin has a look in his eyes that I can't quite place at first, but I'm shocked when I recognize it. That must be how I look at Nell too.

"Hey, don't get any ideas in your head." Nell smiles. "I see that look on your face."

I feel Sandy's hand around my wrist. He knows I might do something dumb at any moment.

"I'm not getting any ideas," Martin says, smiling back. "But I do want you to be careful. Those guys are there for a reason."

"I know," says Nell. "And you're right."

Their words slowly get through to me. This is about our housing complex, about Sandy, about *me*.

"Can I tell you something?"

Martin nods. "Of course."

"Promise you won't just explode?"

"I'll do my best."

Nell takes a deep breath. "I was talking to a boy this week. He hasn't lived with his parents for a while now, and I think he's had a really hard time."

This is about me. I want to put my fingers in my ears, but at the same time I want to hear everything.

"We talk a lot. I like him."

I feel a smile on my lips.

"You like him?" I can hear the jealousy in Martin's voice.

"Yes, he's always so friendly. Actually, he's the one who suggested we should both quit smoking."

That was Nell's idea, but I don't care. I feel like I'm floating.

"He sometimes confides in me, about things that happened in the past. His parents died in a car accident, and he was bullied a lot when he was first placed in care."

"This is about that Kelly, isn't it?"

"Exactly."

My heart thumps hopefully against the tree trunk. So they've talked about me before. What does that mean? I'm on Nell's mind—that much is clear. Maybe that's why Martin's so jealous.

"But what did you want to tell me?"

Nell hesitates for a moment. "Well, at the beginning of this week, something strange happened. When I was talking to him, I got this weird feeling."

Did she feel the same as me? I was right. Nell likes me as much as I like her. That dumb Martin—he thinks he's in with a chance. He's too late. She's already mine.

"Weird? How do you mean?"

"Well, he was telling me about how he ended up in care. Said he'd done something terrible. That he destroyed someone's life because he thought he had every right to." Nell pauses. "It wasn't even what he said. It was the way he said it. The look in his eyes was so dark. I was scared of him."

I feel Sandy's hand tighten around my wrist.

"I understand. What happened then?"

"I wanted to run away, but I didn't dare."

Inside my body, something breaks. I feel shards swirling through me, all the way down to my feet.

"So what did you do?"

"I just said we all sometimes do stuff we're not proud of. Luckily that dark look in his eyes disappeared then, and I was able to get away."

Sandy curses quietly.

"You did the right thing."

"Do you think so?"

"Of course."

"You're so sweet."

"Oh, I am, am I?"

"Of course you are." I can hear Nell smiling as she says, "Don't look at me like that."

"Like what?"

"You know what I mean."

"Does it bother you?"

"Maybe not . . ."

••••

Branches whip my face. I stumble and fall, hitting my knee on something hard.

"Kelly!" Sandy's voice sounds a long way off. "Wait."

I was scared of him.

Everything Nell said to me, everything she did—it was all one big lie. Why didn't I see that?

I need to break something.

I need to hit someone.

I need to hurt someone.

"Kelly." Sandy drops down next to me on the ground and puts his arms around me.

"She's lying!"

"I know."

"She was different, Sandy."

"I know."

"I really thought . . ."

"It's okay." Sandy hugs me close. His arms feel safe and strong. I'm too tired to resist and I lean my whole weight against him.

"That girl can drop dead. Right?"

I nod.

After a while, Sandy lets me go. "You okay now?"

I nod, but I feel drained, like I've just been through a tough therapy session.

"There's no way you could have known, Kelly."

That's the problem. I *should* have known. Sandy's been warning me about her all night, but I kept on sticking up for Nell. Nell was different from the other neighbors. Nell saw me as Kelly, not as some problem case.

In reality, she's terrified of me.

"That Martin's an asshole." Sandy cracks his fingers. "He thinks he's better than us."

I look at my friend. "You still got that knife?"

"Why?"

"We might need it."

Sandy raises his eyebrows. "What are you planning to do? Stab that Martin guy?"

You did the right thing.

Do you think so?

Of course.

You're so sweet.

That Martin must be laughing at me. He has Nell wrapped around his little finger with his sweet talk, and he barely needed to try. All he had to do was be normal. If I'd been born into a different family, it could have been me standing there now with Nell.

"You can't stab anyone," says Sandy when I don't reply. "You're way too good for that."

"How do you know?"

"I've known you long enough."

"I don't want to be good anymore," I say. "It doesn't get me anywhere. Give me that knife."

Sandy carefully takes it from his pocket. "Are you sure you—"

I snatch it from his hands. The knife's heavier than I'd expected. I see my reflection in the blade. Slowly, I turn the knife over and over in my hands. The scars on my face move as it turns. Then I hand it back to him.

"You hang on to this for now. Was she scared?" I ask quietly.

A shadow passes over Sandy's face. He immediately knows what I'm talking about.

"Not at first," he says. "She was in the kitchen when I went to see her. I don't think she even saw the knife. She only ever thought about herself. When I held out the knife, she just started yelling and calling me names. Said I was a failure. With me standing there, pointing a knife at her. Stupid bitch."

"What happened then?"

"I poked her in the gut with the tip of the knife." Sandy leans forward, grabs my hand with the knife in it, and brings it to a point just above his navel. "Here."

I realize I'm holding my breath as he continues the story.

"She still thought she could control me. So I pushed a bit harder."

Sandy pulls my hand even closer. I feel his skin tighten under the tip of the knife.

"She asked if I needed money. Like that was what it was about. I wanted her to say sorry. I just wanted to hear her say that, even if it was only once."

I understand. I don't think anyone understands Sandy better than I do.

"And did she?"

"Of course she didn't." Sandy lets go of my hand. "She doesn't regret anything at all."

"And what did you do then?"

"You know that story."

I look at Sandy's hand. His burn is still gruesomely obvious, even in the flashlight's dim glow.

He's right. I do know the story. Sandy grabbed a lighter and set the kitchen curtains on fire.

His mother got out in time, and she held the kitchen door closed from the outside by throwing all her weight against it. She locked Sandy in.

Sandy managed to escape into the yard—but he had to go through the burning curtains to get there. He had third-degree burns on his hand, which has never completely healed.

"We're going to do it," I say firmly. "We'll show them we're not just a couple of problem kids. From now on, we'll never let them walk all over us again."

Sandy's eyes are gleaming. "What's your plan?"

I turn the knife in my hand. "We're taking over Fright Night."

MURDERER

That was the point where it all started going really wrong.
I wasn't thinking clearly.
No one was thinking clearly.

DYLAN

"Dylan!" Quin's voice sounds close. I slip behind a tree and lean against the trunk. I'm panting.

"I'm sorry about your glasses. I didn't mean to do it. But why did you get so mad?"

I can feel the photo and the postcard poking my thigh through my pocket. If Sofia was in my old house, maybe she saw some other stuff. What does she know about Mom?

She was asking all those questions for a reason. She wanted to see if I'd tell the truth. I've lied to her a few times—and she knows.

But I thought she wanted to come meet Mom because she cares about me. I bite the inside of my cheek.

"Dylan?"

Quin is going to stay there until it gets light. He's being so very kind that it's irritating me.

"Get the hell away from me."

I hear Quin take a few steps toward me.

"And what then? You going to go home?"

The volcano inside me is rumbling dangerously.

"That's *your* home, not mine. My bedroom isn't even mine. It's your dad's study. I stole it."

Quin sighs. "Are you starting that again?"

He doesn't get it. He really doesn't get it.

"Leave me alone, Quin."

"I'm not going back without you. You're my brother."

I push my back against the tree trunk.

"*Brother*? We're not brothers, Quin. I don't have a brother! You're a friend I have to live with, and it drives me crazy! Do you know I still ask for permission when I want to grab some juice from the fridge? And that I don't spend the night in my own room because I can't sleep a wink in there? Why do you think I always fold and put away my own clothes? If Hester did it, nothing at all would be like it was before. She cooks such a big meal every night that it's like royalty's coming to dinner. She makes my lunch, and she asks how my day at school was. She and Johan are always there, keeping their eagle eyes on me. And you? You act like it's all one big fun sleepover. But I've lost everything. And I hate it. I hate your house!"

My last sentence echoes through the woods. I don't mean it, but at the same time I do. I listen to the silence. Ten, twenty, thirty seconds. And then I hear Quin's footsteps again. This time they're walking away from me.

KELLY

"We have to be quick." Sandy points at the big tree with the luminous arrow on it.

Nell and Martin are still nearby. The girl I don't know is standing with her back to us. What will she do if she sees us?

"I'll do it," I say quietly.

"You sure?" Sandy's almost invisible now that our flashlight is off.

"Certain."

I walk quickly to the big tree, keeping my eyes on the girl's back. If she turns around now . . .

I grab hold of the arrow and turn it around. Instead of pointing right, the thing's pointing left now, away from the path.

Will they suspect anything? No. No one expects us here. No one expects something like this to happen.

And by the time the group realizes what's going on, it'll be too late.

DYLAN

It feels like I've been walking for hours. I haven't seen any actors for a while. Or heard other Fright Nighters screaming.

Where should I go? Hester and Johan won't understand why I'm coming back on my own. They'll fire all kinds of questions at me, and I'll only get myself into more trouble. Plus, I said some horrible things about them. Of course I'm happy they took me into their family, or I'd be in some kind of home or institution, like those kids at Nell's work.

"Ow!"

I bump into something. At first I think it's a tree, but then my fingers feel something else. A fence! This must be the edge of the woods.

I walk along the fence for a bit, but it doesn't end. So I'll have to go over it. I put my sneaker against the slippery bars and pull myself up.

I'm feeling the effects of my fight with Quin; there's a stabbing pain in my ribs. I drop down on the other side of the fence. It's asphalt, but it's not the bike path we took to get here.

So it looks like I'm on the other side of the woods. If I want to get back to the bikes, I'll have to walk a really long way. Getting a taxi isn't an option, because all my stuff is inside a locker at the start. And I don't have a cent on me.

I slide onto the ground and lean back against the fence. If I have to, I'll sit here until it gets light. In a few hours, some dog owner is bound to walk past.

But then what?

There's no way I can go back to Quin, not after everything I said to him. I massage my painful right leg, then drop my face into my hands. It's pitch dark. And I just gave one friend a bloody nose and terrified the other with my yelling.

Then I feel something against my chest. I reach under my T-shirt and close my hand around the key. For the first time since finding Sofia's jacket, I feel something like hope.

There *is* somewhere I can go.

SOFIA

Martin and Nell come back.

"Are they still not here?" Martin says with a sigh. "This is taking way too long."

He's so annoying. It's like Fright Night is all that matters. Has he forgotten everything that just happened?

"Let's wait a few more minutes," suggests Nell.

Shocked, I stare at her. "And what then? There's no way I'm leaving without them!"

"We don't have to." Nell points at something behind me. "Someone's coming."

I turn around and see Quin walking up—on his own.

"Where's Dylan?"

Quin looks deathly pale, except for the marks left by his nosebleed.

"He didn't want to come back." Quin's voice sounds weary.

"What happened?" I put my arms around him and feel his shaking hands on my waist. "Did you guys fight again?"

"No . . . he's just really mad."

125

Quin's voice cracks. Big, brave Quin, who's never lost for words, starts crying. I hug him closer.

"It's not you," I whisper. "I don't know what's going on either, but I'm sure Dylan didn't want to hurt you."

Quin mutters something I don't hear and twists out of my hug. Wildly, he wipes his eyes dry.

"Let's go on," he says.

I gape at him. "What?!"

Martin slaps him on the shoulder. "You sure?"

"Absolutely certain."

"You're kidding, aren't you?" I look toward where Dylan disappeared. "He's out there on his own somewhere."

"So what?" Suddenly there's nothing left of Quin's tears, and his face is hard. "That's his choice."

"We can't leave him behind."

"He left *us* behind," Quin says. "And he was very clear about it."

I look at Nell, but she just shrugs.

"Okay, then," says Martin, turning to look at the big tree behind him. "We have to go left here."

"Left?" I look at the path, which clearly heads right. "Are you sure?"

"We're going off-road for a bit," says Quin. "That's cool."

Martin and Quin lead the way. I pause at the tree.

"Dylan will be fine," says Nell. "He's probably waiting for us at the exit."

I want to believe Nell, but my gut says something different. If we continue now, it's like we're abandoning Dylan.

126

I look at the big tree in front of me. Maybe he'll come back here, to the place where we last saw each other. I have to leave something behind for him, some kind of message. There's a branch sticking out next to the arrow. It's perfect.

I take the bracelet off my wrist and hang it on the branch.

...

"Where have all the actors gone?" says Quin after a while. We're walking straight through the woods. Sometimes Martin has to hold big branches aside for us so we can get through.

"It's nice and peaceful," says Nell. "I'm so done with this Fright Night."

"And then, just when you least expect it . . . ," says Martin with a grin.

"Yeah," says Quin. "Any minute now someone's going to leap out of the bushes!"

"How can you guys be so casual?" I think about my bracelet on the tree. What if Dylan doesn't come back? What if something happens to him in the woods? He could easily fall, with that leg of his.

"What do you want us to do? Start crying and wailing?" Quin stops walking. "Like I said, it was his choice, not ours."

"It's like you don't care."

Quin's eyes narrow. "Dylan's my best friend. Of course I care."

"He's in trouble. We have to help him."

"He went crazy," says Quin. "That's a completely different story."

"If you ask me, he's terrified. That's why he lies about everything."

Quin raises one surprised eyebrow. "Lying? What? Dylan doesn't lie."

"Well, he lied about his mom. He said she lives at home, but that's not true. And he lies about his leg."

Quin sighs. "His leg again? What about it?"

I look at Nell. "Dylan told her it was a hockey accident, but he told me that he fell off his bike."

Quin's face clouds over.

"What?" I take hold of his arm. "What is it?"

"Nothing. Let's keep going."

"Please stop protecting him. I need to know what's going on. He constantly avoids the truth—haven't you noticed?"

Quin gives a deep sigh. "Okay. Fine. Neither story's true."

"What do you mean?"

"There's another version. The version he told me at the time."

I feel my eyes widening. "And what's that?"

"Dylan fell down the stairs. That's why he walks with a limp."

DYLAN

Nothing has changed, but at the same time everything is different.

The streetlights cast yellow patches on the ground every few yards. I stop in front of number 12. It's like the house is waiting for us to come back but secretly knows it's not going to happen.

The front yard is overgrown with weeds. Mom would hate to see it like that. I bend down and pull a few plants from between the slabs. So Sofia was here a few days ago. How did she get inside?

I tilt back my head and look up. Behind the windows upstairs, the curtains are closed as usual.

"I don't want anyone snooping." Mom closes the curtains. It's suddenly a lot darker in my room. She never noticed that I'd swapped her old glasses.

I see that Mom is all dolled up. She's wearing her favorite red lipstick, black pantyhose, and her high-heeled boots.

"Are you going to a party?" I ask.

"No, we have an appointment. We have to drive a long way this time, but that's okay. Because the doctor at this new hospital is definitely going to find out what's up with you."

A new hospital? This is a shock.

"What about Eliza? She's my doctor, isn't she?"

"Are you going to start crying?"

I feel tears burning my eyes, and I desperately try to keep them in. But when I shake my head, they come pouring out.

"But I like Eliza."

"You don't have to like her. She's not your friend." Mom pulls me up by my arms. "Get up and come with me."

My legs feel like lead. I lie on my bed like a rag doll.

"Dylan!" Mom glares at me. "Come on!"

I want to, but I really can't move. It's like my legs are rebelling.

"G-give me a moment."

"Does it hurt?"

"No, no, no . . ." I'm sweating. Mom is going to think my legs are sick. I need them to work—and now.

"Stop messing with me, Dylan!" Mom slaps my cheek hard. "You had better make sure you cooperate with the new doctor. I don't want you showing me up! You hear me?"

I take the key from around my neck and put it in the lock. The front door swings open.

In front of me, I see the familiar wooden stairs. As usual, a shiver goes through me when I see the steps. I still remember how it felt when I fell down each and every one of them. There are a few envelopes on the mat, all addressed to Mom. Bills, advertisements, a reminder for a dental appointment. Should I take the mail for her tomorrow?

I look up. The mirror in the hallway shows my face. I see some blood on my forehead. Is it mine or Quin's?

I hang the key back around my neck and close the front door. Now it really is quiet. It's like a ghost house here in the dark. I walk to the living room and turn on the light. The bright light flooding the room startles me, so I turn it off. The last thing I need now is for one of the neighbors to call the police because they think someone's breaking in. Anyway, I have enough light from the lampposts outside. It's way less dark here than at Fright Night.

I walk through the living room and run my hand over the piano. In the kitchen I fill a glass with water. It's only now that I realize how thirsty I am. My mouth still tastes like cockroach too.

In two gulps, I empty the glass and then I fill it again. The cold water makes my head clearer. There's just a photo frame left on the windowsill. Sofia took the photo. It's like there's been a burglar in here. None of the stuff feels like mine anymore, not now that I know Sofia's been touching it.

What was she doing here? It's no wonder she looked guilty when I showed her the photo and asked her about my room. She had no right to be in there—and she knows that. Did she go into my old bedroom here too? I open the door to the hallway again. At the bottom of the stairs I feel my legs go limp, but I still place my foot on the first step.

When I reach the top, the first thing I do is open the bathroom door. The bathroom's smaller than I remember. At Quin's, they have a separate shower and bath. Here we just have a shower, with a tiny washbasin. The washing machine is positioned so that you have to squeeze past it sideways to step into the shower. But it's clean. Even now. Did Mom ask Gerda to look after the place?

I think about our old neighbor, who used to chat with Mom. She was crazy about Mom and always paid her compliments. I'd hear her voice downstairs when I was stuck in bed yet again: *Oh, Dylan's so lucky to have such a caring mom.*

Ah, of course, it was Gerda who let Sofia in! She's the only one with a key. What if she told Sofia things about me? Gerda's such a gasbag—she always knew all the neighborhood gossip. Maybe Sofia knows even more than I feared.

Quickly, I close the bathroom door behind me and look at the door to my bedroom. Behind that door is my familiar refuge, the place where I could hide away. The place that ultimately changed into my prison, shut off from the outside world. Should I really go in there?

But then I think about tonight. Everything's gone to pieces. How much worse can it get?

I push down the door handle.

It takes a moment for my eyes to get used to the dark, but then I see my bed, with the striped comforter. On the

132

ceiling there are still those sticky stars I was really too old for, but still I left them there. And I see my desk with the stack of comics, which I know inside out. After all, I had plenty of time to read.

"Great," Mom says, looking around the room. "This is perfect."

The curtains are closed and I am lying on the bed. On my back, dead still, like Mom wanted.

She had a very long conversation with the new doctor, and he was going to run some tests because my muscle strength had decreased so much. The tests were going to start next week. Mom was so happy that she'd bought me an ice cream from the hospital lobby. Strawberry and chocolate, my favorite flavors.

Back in my bedroom, she'd tucked me in really tightly, so I could hardly move. She'd been doing that a lot lately. I lie there now, packed up like a mummy for days on end.

"Dr. Luiting says you're not allowed to leave your bed."

Dr. Luiting is nowhere near as nice as Eliza. I wasn't allowed to call him by his first name, and his eyes didn't sparkle. He said he thought Mom was very smart.

Mom bought loads of books with tricky titles, all about being sick. Luckily I have my own comic books to read. That makes the days pass a bit faster.

I long to be outside, though, to feel the fresh wind on my face. I even long to be back at school, because then I'd see Quin again. Mom says I can't go to school for a while, though.

She even sent away Sven, who came to ask if I wanted to play soccer.

"I'm interested to hear what Dr. Luiting will have to say next week."

Mom looks at the tight comforter with a satisfied smile. "You know, I think you've taken another turn for the worse."

I nod obediently, because since I've started doing that, Mom has stopped hitting me.

SOFIA

"F-fell down the stairs?" I stammer.

Quin turns around. "Can we continue?"

"But . . . how?"

"You know, he just fell." Quin sighs, like I'm a little kid who doesn't understand the rules of a game.

"Why would he lie about it?"

"No idea. Why does it matter?"

How can Quin be so laid-back? He just found out that Dylan told three different versions of a story!

"I think Dylan's been through some really bad stuff."

Quin bursts out laughing. "What gave you that idea?"

"His neighbor told me he'd spent months in bed."

Quin frowns. "Gerda? You spoke to her?"

"I went to his house. She let me in."

"Dylan was sick for a while, that's true. Sometimes he didn't come to school for weeks."

"So what was wrong with him?"

"The doctors didn't know exactly. Something with his muscles."

"Didn't you ever ask him about it?"

"When Dylan was at school, he just wanted to be normal. To play soccer and stuff."

I exchange a look with Nell. "If you ask me, you only know half the story, Quin."

"What are you talking about? I know Dylan way better than you do—and I've known him longer too. You weren't there the first night he couldn't sleep at my house. You weren't there when he woke up screaming every night. Do you have any idea how hard it is for him not to live at home?"

Quin's comments hurt. He's right. They have a shared past I'll never be a part of.

"That's all it is. You're just being paranoid," finishes Quin.

"I think Sofia's right," says Nell. "I live with kids like that. I'd recognize that kind of behavior anywhere."

"Dylan isn't crazy!"

Nell makes a soothing sound. "I'm not saying he is. But he attacked you tonight like you were his archenemy. Do you think that's normal?"

Quin doesn't reply.

"Why is it that Dylan lives with you?" asks Nell.

Quin shrugs. "Because his mom's sick."

I nod. "She has cancer."

"No. It's something mental." Quin says it and then falls silent. I can see on his face that he's beginning to understand the knots Dylan has tied himself into. "Of course he said it was cancer. Like he's going to go around telling everyone his mom's gone mad."

It feels like someone's standing on my chest with their entire weight. "I'm not everyone, am I?"

Quin doesn't reply.

"Was his mom a danger to him?"

"Of course not." Quin shakes his head. "If anything, she was overprotective. She was always at the hospital with him, sometimes a few times a week. His mom was crazy about him."

I think about the photo from the windowsill. "They don't seem too close in that photo."

"Photo? You mean the one Dylan showed us?"

I nod.

"You have no idea . . ." Quin pauses for a second. "The boy in that photo isn't Dylan."

DYLAN

I sit down on the edge of my bed. The pressure of the mattress feels so familiar. How many hours have I spent lying here? I had to lie in this bed for days, as my muscles grew weaker and weaker.

I drop back and lie down. It feels exactly like it used to. I see my old ceiling. I know every lump and bump. I can trace every little crack. I gave a name to every sticky star. The biggest one of all was called Quin.

What went wrong tonight? I gave Quin a bloody nose. Feels like I don't know myself at all.

But Quin has no idea what it was like being here, in this bed, with my mom hovering around. He has Hester, and she's the exact opposite of Mom. Hester's a nice woodstove that makes you warm and rosy-cheeked. Mom's like an open fire that burns you.

How am I ever going to explain that to him?

When I finally went back to school, I didn't want to talk about home. I couldn't. If Mom found out I'd confided in Quin . . . So we played soccer, the best medicine. Until even that stopped working. My muscles kept letting me down.

I quickly tense my legs, and then my arms. I clench my

fists and my jaw. Then I let everything go and relax again. My body's almost back to normal, all except for my right leg. Dr. Luiting says the fracture will never completely heal.

I fall down twelve steps.

At the bottom of the stairs, I feel a sharp pain in my right leg. When I look at it, I wished I hadn't. It's like my leg is made of clay. It is twisted at a weird angle.

My first reaction is relief. This time I don't have to pretend. But then I start screaming.

Mom comes hurrying downstairs and crouches beside me. "We have to go to the hospital."

I stand up and walk to the last door: Mom's room. When I was little, I spent lots of time in there, but in recent years it had been off-limits. What does it look like now?

I swing the door open and for a moment it's like she's standing there in front of me. I can vaguely smell her perfume, which she always put on when we went to the hospital. I even catch myself glancing over my shoulder to make sure she's not standing behind me. But the landing's empty.

I look at the pale-green bedspread, which strangely reminds me of the hospital.

A long time ago, she sometimes let me climb into bed with her early on a Sunday morning, but the memory's so vague that I've started to wonder if it's real.

139

As I step through the doorway, I feel pressure on my chest. What am I doing here? What do I hope to achieve? I walk to the bed and sit down. I feel something jab my thigh and take out Sofia's postcard. The blue lake on the front takes my breath away for the second time tonight.

When I turn over the postcard, I see thick black letters.

ONE DAY I'M GOING TO KILL YOU.

The photo had distracted me before. I hadn't seen the words. Did Sofia take the postcard from this house, like the photo? That means it was meant for me or Mom. But who sent it?

Somewhere inside my head, a door opens with an answer behind, but it only opens a crack.

"No," I say quietly. "It can't be . . ."

I stand up and walk back to the landing. At the top of the stairs, I pause. There are the twelve steps leading down, but there's also another staircase.

The stairs to the attic.

I look up, into that dark hole. No, I don't want to go there. That chapter's closed, over. But when I want to go downstairs, my right leg stays where it is. It's like it's forcing me to go up-stairs. No matter what I try, I can't walk downstairs.

"Okay," I say quietly. "You win."

For the first time, my right leg cooperates. It even seems to be moving faster than my left one. Before I know it, I'm up in the attic, where it's even darker than downstairs. My eyes refuse to get used to the dark here, and I need to turn on the light. I run my hand over the wall until I find the switch. The attic fills with bright fluorescent light.

I hold a hand in front of my eyes and peer through my fingers. There are all kinds of things piled up against the slanting wall. Overnight bags, my old high chair, a large supply of detergent, and some moving boxes containing Mom's clothes. There's no sign that this was ever a bedroom.

Or is there?

In a few places, there are stray strips of tape with torn-off corners of paper. That's where the posters were, which Mom must have pulled off the wall.

I feel my heartbeat speed up as I take the photograph from my pocket. The fold in it splits their faces in two. Why did Mom leave it on the windowsill? Did she miss him? Or was it to torture me?

I swipe my finger over his pale face. Some days he looked worse than me, even though Mom left him alone.

Because she had chosen me.

Me.

But why? Because I was the youngest?

I drop down onto the floor; it feels dusty. And then, like someone has pressed a button, I start to cry. I cry the tears that have been in there for years but were never allowed to come out.

This attic is where he slept.

My brother.

SOFIA

"Dylan doesn't have a brother," I say. "That's impossible."

The boy in the photo is Dylan's double.

"Yes, he does," says Quin. "An older brother."

"How . . ." I search for words, but I can't find any.

Nell puts her arm around me. Quin looks uncomfortable.

"As far as Dylan's concerned, he doesn't exist. That's why he never talks about him."

"So what happened? Please, tell me."

Quin cracks his fingers. "It all went wrong at home, so Dylan's brother lives somewhere else now."

"Where?"

Quin shakes his head. "I don't know if I . . ."

"Just tell us," Nell says. "I don't think it matters now."

"He was taken away by social services."

My head's spinning. It's like I don't even know Dylan anymore. How can he have kept this secret all this time?

"Was it because of his mom's sickness?" asks Nell.

Quin shakes his head. "No, no, not at all. Kelly went off the rails all by himself."

It's like the ground underneath me has turned into quicksand. I've already heard that name tonight.

"Kelly?" Nell's voice falters. "Is Dylan's brother called Kelly?"

Quin smiles. "Yeah, I know. It's a girl's name."

At that moment, two figures loom out of the darkness. One is a clown with yellow lenses in his eyes, and next to him is a boy with scars on his face. It looks like he's been attacked by a wild animal.

The clown laughs. "Finally! There you are."

MURDERER

If that knife hadn't been there, everything
would have turned out fine.
But the knife *was* there.

KELLY

Nell is here, right in front of me. As usual, my heart starts beating faster, even now that I know what she thinks about me.

I look her right in the eyes. I have to see if she recognizes me. But she doesn't. Of course she doesn't.

"Follow us." Sandy leads the way. He already told me about the bunker in the woods. It's the perfect place, far enough away from Fright Night. Sandy often used to sleep there to get away from his mom. He says we should have no problem getting in.

When no one was watching, I went back and turned the arrow to the right. We don't want anyone to come along and spoil our fun, do we?

I walk along at the back of the group. Nell is deep in conversation with the other girl, who seems to be trying to calm her down.

"Maybe it's someone else with the same name," I hear the girl saying.

I have no idea what they're talking about, but I don't care. I can't take my eyes off Nell and Martin. Those two think they're safe, but they have no idea who's behind them. Wearing this makeup gives me such a feeling of power. I can do anything to them—and they won't have a clue that it's me.

"Hey, which zone is this?" I hear the other boy ask. He's younger than Martin and he looks vaguely familiar. His face is covered with dried blood. Has he been fighting?

"There's no talking in this zone," Sandy warns him.

I feel a smile on my lips. I could never have done this without him. I know I can count on Sandy. He'll never let me down like Nell did tonight.

Suddenly I feel ashamed for letting Nell say such negative things about Sandy. Who does she think she is?

"I've never met such a grumpy clown," I hear Martin say.

Sandy stops abruptly and looks at Martin. "What was that?"

"I just said you seem pretty cranky for a clown."

For a moment, I think Sandy's going to take out his knife, but then he says, "Believe me, I can be way crankier than this. Now keep walking."

. . .

"We're here."

A concrete bunker looms up in front of us, weather-beaten and covered in ivy. Lit up by our flashlight, the place looks eerie—the perfect setting for our Fright Night finale.

"Now are you finally going to tell us what zone this is?" asks Martin.

Sandy pushes against the wooden door, which swings open, as promised. "In there."

Martin crosses his arms. "I asked you a question."

Sandy goes and stands right in front of him. He shines his flashlight straight into Martin's eyes. "And I said, in there."

"Marty . . ." Nell takes hold of Martin's arm. "Come on."

I look at the small gesture. The rings on her fingers, except for her ring finger. What would it feel like if Nell touched me like that? She even has a pet name for him.

Then they go into the bunker. The entrance is low, and I have to duck so I don't bang my head. It smells of mold and wet dog. So this is where Sandy spent so many nights on his own. I feel a pang of sympathy. Maybe he had an even harder time than me. At least I had my own attic, my own little island.

Don't think about that. I press my fingertips to my temples. The psychologist says it helps to bring you back to the here and now.

Sandy closes the wooden door behind us and puts down the flashlight on some kind of oil barrel in the corner of the room.

"We've come to the best bit of Fright Night now. You might think the worst is behind you, but you're about to find out that nothing could be further from the truth."

The boy sniffs. "One of us ate a cockroach."

"And which one of you was that?" asks Sandy.

"He's not with us now." The girl looks at her sneakers. "We lost someone."

So, there was a fifth team member? Of course, every team has to have five people.

"What I mean is, we've seen some stuff." The boy crosses his arms defiantly.

The girl nudges him. "Quin . . ."

Quin? My gaze shoots to the boy with the bloody nose. I knew I recognized him from somewhere! He's older, of course. I haven't seen him for years.

My hands are tingling. I look around, as if his other half might be hiding here somewhere.

Because wherever Quin went, Dylan went too. My little brother. I press my fingertips to my temples again, but it doesn't help. Questions are shooting through my mind.

What is Dylan's best friend doing here?

And where's Dylan?

That girl was talking about them having lost someone. Was that Dylan? I have to tell Sandy, but how can I do that with everyone here?

"Okay," Sandy continues. "Are we having fun yet?"

Martin glares at him. "It stinks in here."

"That's my home you just insulted." Sandy goes and stands in front of Martin. "You don't want to do that, my friend."

"I'm not your friend." Martin stands up straight. He is way taller than Sandy, but that doesn't seem to bother Sandy.

"No, you're not." Sandy looks him in the eye. His yellow lenses flicker. "You're . . . the opposite of that."

I see Martin hesitate. His shoulders slump a little as he asks, "What are we actually doing here? Which zone is this?"

Sandy gives him a shove. "Why do you keep going on about zones? This isn't any kind of zone."

Martin's eyes shoot to the exit. It's like he only just realized the door is shut.

"You are going to take us back to that arrow right now." Martin's voice is trembling—and that makes me feel so good. Finally, he's scared.

"What arrow? You mean the arrow that we"—Sandy makes a gesture with his hand—"turned around?"

SOFIA

Martin gapes at Sandy. "Turned around?"

The clown laughs. "You still don't get it, do you?"

An anxious feeling creeps over me. It's not the typical Fright Night feeling. This is something else. It has to do with that clown's grin and his silent friend. This doesn't feel right at all.

"We quit," I say firmly. "Ketchup."

There's silence for a moment. They have to stop now. Those are the rules. I can't wait to get back to our bikes. This is the first and last Fright Night of my life. I'm never going to do anything like this again.

But then the clown starts chuckling. "Ketchup? Did you say 'ketchup'?"

"It's the safe word," I say, but my voice sounds small. Why won't they listen?

Martin makes a run for the door, but the clown blocks his way.

"Let us out."

"No."

"Give me your walkie-talkie."

"Why should I?"

Martin clenches his fist. "I'll knock you down if I have to."

The clown just grins. "You can try."

Martin swipes at him. It all happens in a split second, but then I hear someone groan. Did he hit the clown?

Then I see that Martin's the one who's collapsing. He's clasped his hand around his forearm, and his face is twisted. There's a trickle of blood seeping between his fingers. It's like watching a scene from a horror movie. What's happening?!

Then I see the knife. The clown's wiping the blood off the blade with the sleeve of his jacket. He just stabbed Martin!

Nell runs to her friend. "What did you do?!"

"It's just a bit of blood." The clown looks down at them. "And he started it."

He sounds emotionless, like he stabs people every day. I rush forward to help Nell. Together, we help Martin down to the ground. The blood is still pouring through his fingers.

"You have to apply pressure to the wound," I hear myself say. "Here."

I take off my jacket and wrap it around Martin's arm. When I tie a firm knot in it, he groans. The fabric slowly turns red.

"Good, now we can continue." The clown looks at us. "We're here because of Nell."

I see a shock go through her body.

"You aren't going anywhere, Nell," hisses Martin.

I look at the clown and the boy with the scars. Who are they? Are they from Fright Night? Or from somewhere else? They must have deliberately lured us here. They must have turned the arrow around while I was waiting for Quin. I was thinking so much about Dylan and their fight that I wasn't paying attention. We followed them like little sheep because we thought it was part of Fright Night—and now there's no way out.

Frantically, I calculate our odds. There are four of us, and only two of them. But Martin's injured, Quin's a bit puny, and Nell seems terrified. Besides, they're armed and we're not.

"Fine. If Nell doesn't want to cooperate"—the clown points his knife at me—"then you're next."

DYLAN

I'm startled by a shrill sound. The doorbell echoes around the house, all the way up into the attic.

I sit up on the dusty floor and feel my heart pounding as the bell rings again. Someone's at the door, but who could it be?

I slip the photo of Mom and Kelly back into my pocket, and, my heart thumping away, I creep back downstairs. Through the glass in the front door, I see a small, stocky silhouette. It bends down, and the mail slot opens.

"Hello?"

I recognize that voice.

"Gerda?"

"Who's there?"

I slide the bolt and open the door. Gerda's standing in our front yard in striped pajamas and white slippers. She looks at me like I'm a ghost.

"Dylan?"

Before I can even nod, she's wrapped her arms around me. She hugs me tight and I smell her familiar scent. She smells just like her house: of caramel and old people.

Gerda lets go and looks at me. "I got up for a glass of water and saw the lights on. I'm so glad to see you again, young man."

•••

"There's only water," I say, taking a fresh glass from the cabinet.

"Doesn't matter." Gerda sits down at the kitchen table, in the place that was once Kelly's. "You look good."

Even after Fright Night, it seems I look healthier than I did back then.

Dr. Luiting says it's a miracle I survived the fall. I don't want to think about that, but it feels like he's written the words on my plaster cast in permanent marker.

"Thanks."

"I met your girlfriend the other day. Sofia, isn't it?"

I place the glass of water in front of her. "She's just a friend."

Gerda ignores my comment. "She's such a nice girl."

I intertwine my fingers. So they talked—I knew it. I bet Sofia asked her all kinds of questions about me. That thought makes me mad again.

"She was so positive about you."

"Yeah, sure," I say abruptly.

"She told me she felt really lonely at the start of this school year and that you put her at ease. She cares about you—that's pretty clear." Gerda smiles. "No need to look so surprised!"

"You must have misunderstood," I mumble. "Sofia doesn't care about me."

"You sure?" Gerda leans forward. "Then why is she going to so much trouble for a gift?"

"A gift?"

Gerda puts her hand over her mouth. "Oh, shoot. Did I spoil a surprise? I'm so dumb. I just meant the photo album she's making for you."

A photo album? What is this about?

"I hope you don't mind, but I told her to take that photo of your mom and Kelly."

I feel the blood rush to my head. So Sofia didn't just decide to take the photo herself. It was Gerda's suggestion. She was trying to do something nice for me and I exploded at her. I yelled at her like she was my enemy. And I did exactly the same with Quin. He followed me and tried to make up, but I pushed him away.

I hate your house!

I'm just like Mom. I shut my curtains and keep everyone out. Do I think that makes me safer? But I've never felt as lonely as I do now. Running away from Fright Night was the biggest mistake I could have made.

"Where are you going?" Gerda asks when I stand up.

I take a deep breath. "I have to go back."

● ● ●

155

Out of breath, I run the last few yards. My right leg hurts so much, but I don't care. Just as long as I get there in time. I'm relieved to see Sofia's and Quin's bikes still standing next to mine. So they haven't left yet.

It's busy around the exit, with people shouting enthusiastically and announcements being made. A bunch of girls come running in hysterically. They're all crying and laughing at the same time, and their mascara's running.

"That was awesome!"

"That was horrible!"

I stand on tiptoe and scan the crowd, looking for Martin, who's so tall that he must stick up above everyone. I don't see him, so I squeeze my way through to the exit. There are still groups coming out.

"Hey, excuse me?" I stop a boy. "Which group were you in?"

"Group seventeen. Why?"

So how can they have finished before our group? I must have missed my friends. It's the only explanation.

"Nothing, doesn't matter. Thanks."

I walk around again and check the bikes a second time. Where could Sofia and Quin be? There's no sign of anyone at the restrooms either. Are they waiting for me in the woods?

I pace back and forth near the exit. Now even the actors are coming out. I recognize one of the girls as the actress with the chainsaw. She's deep in conversation with a zombie.

"Great first night," I hear the zombie say.

"Sure was. Someone even asked me on a date."

"Seriously? A Fright Nighter?"

She laughs. "Duh. No. Another actor. That guy with the girl's name . . . Sandy."

"Oh yeah, the creepy one from the training course. I think he was over-identifying with his role."

"I kind of liked him. His friend's looking for a date too."

"You mean the other one with a girl's name?"

The actress with the chainsaw nods. "Kelly."

A strange sound escapes from my throat. I stare after them until they go into the backstage area. Why is my heart thumping so fast? There are other Kellys out there. It doesn't mean it's my brother.

I think about the postcard. What if it really was Kelly who wrote it? Maybe the words weren't meant for Mom at all, but for me. It's no secret that Kelly and I don't get along. There's a reason why he never got in touch after social services took him away. From one day to the next, he disappeared.

Did Kelly know I'd be here tonight? Is that why he signed up as an actor, so that he could be near me anonymously?

I sigh. It feels like I'm losing it. This whole theory makes no sense. I look around again, but there's still no sign of my friends. It's so busy at the exit. There must be at least thirty groups milling around.

Something's not right. I have to go back into the woods.

"Hey, where do you think you're going?" One of the organizers stops me.

"I want to go back in."

The man laughs. "Then you're the only one. Everyone else is glad it's over!"

I shake my head. "You don't get it. My friends are still in there. I—"

"Out is out. You can wait here for them." The man stands in my way and holds out his elbows so I can't get past.

I curse. I'm about to turn around when I hear a shout.

"We've got a fainter!"

The guard hurries over there. "Go get some water! Give the girl some space."

Because of the sudden commotion, no one is paying any attention to me. I grab a flashlight from the returns box and for the second time tonight, I enter Fright Night.

KELLY

Sandy stabbed Martin. It happened so fast that I couldn't stop him.

But would I have stopped him if I could have?

I look at Martin's arm. It's bleeding much less now, thanks to the jacket. Nell is glued to his side. She's stroking his hair. The other girl, who's apparently called Sofia, is standing with her back to the wall and looking at the knife with big eyes.

"What do you want from us?" Quin's hardly said anything, but now he's decided to open his mouth. "Money?"

I saw his mom and dad once at a school play. We shook hands and I could tell right away that they were in a different class. I think Mom noticed, too, because she avoided them all night. I think she was really annoyed that Dylan liked them so much. Whenever he'd been at Quin's place, she'd get all weird and grumpy.

"Not everything is about money," says Sandy.

"Martin has to get out of here." Nell looks at me. "Please, you seem to be the more reasonable one. You can see he needs help, can't you?"

I feel a shiver run down my spine. Nell really has no idea that it's me standing here in front of her. This whole thing was *my* idea, and I'd do it all over again. She shouldn't have lied to me. If she'd been honest, it would never have come to this. But she broke my heart. She gave me hope, but really she was afraid of me. She's the best actress I know.

"I've seen a thing or two. I work with problem kids. I know it can feel like there's no way out, but there's always a way. You don't have to do this. Just let us go."

Is that how she sees me? As work? I'll never get closer to her than this. After tonight, Martin will be the one sitting beside her on the bench. Then I'll be able to see them kissing from my bedroom window.

I walk over to Nell. She shrinks away as I stand in front of her. I study her face. Those little freckles around her nose, her bright-blue eyes, the curve of her lips . . . This is my only chance. With my makeup on, she'll never recognize me. I can do whatever I want.

I lean forward.

SOFIA

He's kissing her. The boy with the scars is putting his disgusting lips on Nell's. Martin tries to get up, but Nell has already given the boy a hard kick on the shin, which makes him let go. He curses and clutches his leg.

The clown grabs Nell by the hair and yanks her back. She screams and nearly loses her balance.

"You dumb bitch! Who do you think you are? You think you can beat us?" The clown smashes Nell into the concrete wall and turns to his friend. "You okay?"

The boy with the scars grins, but there are tears in his eyes.

"That was foolish, very foolish." The clown looks at us all, one by one. "Now you are all going to have to pay."

Martin hugs Nell, who's crying silently. He's supporting his wounded arm, and I can see from his face that he's wishing he could attack them.

Quin wraps his clammy hand around mine. When I look up, I see panic in his eyes. For the first time tonight, Quin is really scared, and there's nothing I can say to reassure him.

We're like rats in a trap.

DYLAN

This is the place where I left the others. The arrow's pointing right, for the final part of Fright Night. I feel a wave of disappointment rush through me. They're not here.

"Quin!" His name echoes around the woods, but I don't hear an answer. "Sofia! Nell! Martin!"

Nothing.

I spin and shine my flashlight around, as if they might be hiding behind a tree somewhere. But I'm all alone.

I'm about to walk on, when something catches my eye. What's that on the branch over there? Right next to the arrow, at eye level, I see Sofia's bracelet. I take it off the branch and run the beads through my fingers. Did she hang it up there for me? Was she trying to tell me something?

I look all around again but see nothing out of the ordinary. So maybe they did just go on walking and they've reached the finish by now. But then I see the footprints in the earth. They're not going right, but left, off the path. I shine my flashlight and see that the footprints go deeper into the woods. Did they turn off here?

I look at the arrow. It makes the most sense to follow it and head right, but something's telling me to go the other way.

Clasping the bracelet, I turn left.

KELLY

"I am going to kill you," I hear Martin muttering. "I am so going to kill you."

It feels like there's a hole in my chest. The pain in my leg is nothing compared to Nell's tears.

I don't understand. This is what I wanted, isn't it? He's bleeding, she's crying—I've had my revenge. So why does it feel like I just lost for the second time tonight?

"If I ever see you outside of this bunker, then—"

"Then what?" Sandy points his knife at Martin. "What's your big plan?"

Martin clenches his jaw.

"Thought so. You're all talk."

I suddenly feel dead tired. I want to go home. I want to sleep. And I want to wake up tomorrow and find that this was all one big nightmare. I want Nell to be waiting for me on the bench and for her to tell me that she wants to go out with me. But what I want most of all is not to want her anymore. Nell is an illusion that is sucking me dry.

Sandy runs the blunt edge of the knife over Martin's cheek.

"No . . ." Nell hiccups through her tears. "Don't. We won't say anything. We won't cause any problems for you."

"People like you always cause problems for us! You think you're better than us." Sandy turns the knife and draws it in one slow movement down Martin's cheek. The blood pours out like berry juice. Martin grimaces, but he doesn't make a sound.

"Stop! Please!" Nell pleads, grabbing Sandy's arm, but he doesn't listen. A pitch-black shadow slides across Sandy's face. That must be how he looked at his mom that time. His mom, who drove him crazy until he really lost it. Years of therapy were supposed to help him—and they did. He finally learned to control himself. Until now. I can see it in his eyes.

"Stop," I say in a hoarse voice, but Sandy raises his knife again.

"Quit it." This time I say it louder.

Sandy finally looks at me. His eyes are wild.

"What's your problem?"

"That's enough," I say quietly.

Sandy shakes his head. "We have to show them who's boss."

"They already know that." I look at Nell, who's as pale as a corpse. Sofia and Quin are still holding hands. We have power over the four of them, but it doesn't help. I feel just as empty as I did before.

"Give me that knife. This has to stop."

Sandy shakes his head. "It'll never stop, Kelly."

My name shivers around the bunker. I see Nell looking through the three layers of makeup.

"K-Kelly?" she stammers. "Is that you?"

SOFIA

Kelly is here. Dylan's brother. I look at his dark eyes again. Now that I know who's standing before me, I recognize the eyes from the photograph.

"How could you . . ." Nell stares at him. She shakes her head slowly, as if that might help the information to fall into the right boxes.

"Leave," says Kelly quietly. "It's over."

"So it was you who kissed her?" Martin's face is ashen. "You are so busted, man. I'll personally ensure you never come anywhere near Nell again."

Kelly ignores him. His eyes are fixed on Nell, who is still shaking her head.

"Go on. Leave."

Why aren't we moving? If this Kelly is offering us a way out, we need to take it.

"There's no need to be scared of me anymore. I won't hurt you."

Kelly's voice is much quieter than before. For a moment, I hear a resemblance to Dylan, and yet I don't want to hear it. I take a quick look at Sandy, who is standing right next to Kelly. Now that he's distracted, we should be able to make it to the door.

Quin pulls my arm and, without thinking, I follow him. He pushes the door open and we almost stumble over each other to get out. The fresh air hits my face as I start running. I count my steps. Five, six, seven . . .

What do we do if they come after us? How does it feel to get a knife in your back? Do you die instantly? Or do you slowly bleed out?

In the distance, I can see a light. Another Fright Nighter?

"Hey!" I shout. "Over here!"

"Help!" calls Nell, from just behind me. "We need help!"

I hear Martin groan. The beam of light is heading our way. It's going way too slowly. I run toward it, with Quin.

"Over here!" I keep shouting. "This way."

The light's very close now.

It feels like my feet leave the ground when I see who it is.

DYLAN

I feel her arms around my neck. Sofia presses her shaking body so tightly to mine that all the air is knocked out of my lungs.

"What happened?" I ask. Her hair tickles my face.

"In the bunker . . . Martin . . . a knife . . . Where *were* you?" Sofia lets go of me and gives my chest a thump.

Quin's face is twisted with fear. "We have to get away from here, as quickly as we can."

"What's going on?" I look behind them. Martin and Nell come running up together. Martin is stumbling, as if every step is an effort. There's a bloody gash on his face and a blood-stained denim jacket wrapped around his arm.

It's Sofia's jacket.

"Wh-what—" I stammer.

"They attacked us." Sofia's voice is trembling. "There's a clown with a knife. And the other one tried to kiss Nell. Your brother's . . ."

"Kelly?" I feel a flaming pain in my chest. So I wasn't going crazy—he really *is* here. Did *he* do that to Martin?

"That friend of his is insane." Sofia takes my hand. "We have to go."

I look at our hands, which fit together perfectly. One day I'll tell her everything. I can trust her. I slip her bracelet back around her wrist and give her my flashlight.

"Here. Follow the path back toward the exit. Get someone to call the police."

Sofia looks at me with big eyes. "What about you?"

I look at the darkness behind her. "Is he in there?"

Quin shakes his head. "You're not going in there. He's dangerous."

"Mom, where's Kelly?"

"Gone." Mom is sitting at the kitchen table, flicking through a magazine.

"Gone? What do you mean?"

"He lives somewhere else now."

I thought about our last conversation in his room. Did it have something to do with that?

Mom turns a page. "Just be glad you're rid of him."

"Guys," Nell pleads, "Martin needs help."

Quin looks back. For a moment, I think he's going to go with them, but then he hands the flashlight to Nell.

"You guys go."

Nell nods gratefully and starts walking. Martin groans with every step he takes.

Bewildered, I look at my friend. "What are you doing?"

"What do you think?"

Sofia nods. "We're going with you."

MURDERER

Did you feel it coming?

DYLAN

The concrete of the bunker feels cold when I hide by the entrance with Quin and Sofia. Angry voices are coming from inside.

"Why did you let them go?"

"It's over, Sandy."

I thought I'd forgotten Kelly's voice, but I recognize it instantly.

"Over? Are you kidding? Do you have any idea what's going to happen now? That bitch is going to report us to the police and we're both going to end up in jail!"

"Then why did you say my name? You were lucky she didn't already recognize your voice!"

He curses. "You should never have lost your head over a neighbor."

"Nell is . . ."

"She's just some *girl,* like billions of others! Wake up, man!"

I feel Sofia's clammy hand in mine. Quin is panting. I'm putting them in danger. This is my fight, not theirs.

"You guys need to go," I whisper.

In the darkness, I just see a glint in Quin's eyes. "Never."

He let me send him away before, but I know he'll stay this time.

"And it's all thanks to your little brother," comes a voice from inside the bunker.

I gasp. This is about me.

"What's Dylan got to do with this?"

There's a sigh. "All the trouble started with him, didn't it?"

Is this about the last conversation I had with Kelly, just before the accident on the stairs?

"You're almost out of medication. I'm just going to go by the pharmacy." Mom puts her head around the door. "Stay in bed, okay?"

I nod obediently.

"See you later."

My bedroom door closes, soon followed by the front door. This is the moment I've been waiting for. This has to come to an end—and Kelly is my only chance.

I frantically kick off the comforter. It isn't easy, because it's so tightly tucked in. I peep around the curtains to make sure she's gone. Mom is heading down the road. Ten minutes is all I have.

I dash out into the hall and up the stairs. I haven't been in his room for ages. I know better than that. Kelly seems to be getting angrier and angrier lately. With Mom, with me, with the world.

"What?" he shouts when I knock on his door.

I swing the door open and see my brother lying on his bed. He raises his eyebrows when he sees me.

"Is the patient out of bed?" he says.

"I have to talk to you." Feeling jumpy, I look over my shoulder. One of my ten precious minutes has already ticked away.

"What about?"

"About Dr. Luiting. About the injections. About Mom."

Kelly sighs. *"What is it this time?"*

"Stop it." Kelly's voice sounds weak.

"Since when do you stick up for him?"

"I'm not. I just don't want to talk about it anymore."

"I'm not sick." It feels like I'm throwing my diary at his feet and yelling, Go on! Read it!

"You're not sick?" Kelly laughs. *"You look like a ghost."*

I look over my shoulder again. How many minutes do I have left?

"I'm pretending. I have to. Like, I don't need glasses. See!"

Kelly looks through my lenses. "Huh?"

I can see from his face that he doesn't have a clue what's going on.

"I don't have a prescription. These are fake. I swapped Mom's old glasses for this pair."

"W-why?" Kelly stammers.

"Because I have to pretend," I say again. *"It's a kind of game. Do you see?"*

A shadow passes over Kelly's face. "A game?"

"Yes, Mom's game."

He swears at me.

Shocked, I look at him. "What?"

He curses again, hitting me with his pillow.

"But . . . ," I say. "You don't understand."

"Go away!" Kelly stands up from his bed and forces me backward. I grab hold of the handrail just in time, or I'd have fallen then and there.

Kelly puts his face right up to mine and in his eyes I see the wild look that has become all too familiar lately.

"I don't want to talk to you. I don't want to see you."

"But—"

"I don't want you to be my brother. I don't want to play soccer with you."

"It's Mom. Mom makes me do it."

The most important words I have ever spoken are drowned in his rage.

"I want you to die!"

I thunder down the stairs, two steps at a time.

"Do you hear me?" Kelly shouts after me. "As far as I'm concerned, you're dead!"

On the landing, at the top of the stairs, I stumble over my own feet—and then go tumbling down.

"He fell. That poor sad little Dylan fell down the stairs. Big deal. Too bad he survived."

My hand slips out of Sofia's.

"He must have laughed so much when you were taken away by social services."

"That's not true!"

It's a moment before I realize that loud voice came out of me. Inside the bunker, everything goes silent, and Sofia and Quin hold their breath too.

I take a step forward, into the bunker. "That is not true."

KELLY

Even before I see him, I know it's him.

"That is not true." Dylan's standing in the doorway. He's tall now and he has to bend his knees to come into the bunker. He still has the same wide mouth and dark eyes, just like mine. It's like looking at an old photo of myself.

Sandy looks like he's seen a ghost. "Dylan?"

I've often wondered what it would be like to see him again. What would I feel? The same rage I felt that afternoon? The grudge I held against him after that? Strangely, I don't feel any of that. It's like everything's gone numb.

"I never laughed." Dylan's voice pulls me back into the bunker. "You were just . . . gone. Mom said it was better that way."

I press my fingertips to my temples, but not even a thousand fingers could help me now.

"You hated me. You sent me away that afternoon, but I just wanted to talk to you."

That part of my life is sealed off, hidden away. All those years of therapy had an effect. I've managed to put things into perspective. I dyed my hair and let it grow. It was time for a new beginning, a new Kelly. I told everyone my mom and dad had died in a car accident. Killed instantly. A simple lie and people never ask any more questions. What else was I supposed to say? That my own mom had thrown me out?

"Why did you hate me so much?"

Dylan's voice sounds just like it used to. Wailing, whining. When I went to the bathroom at night, he was often crying in his room. I never went in, always crept back upstairs.

"Were you that jealous of me?" Dylan looks at me, pleading. "Please, just tell me why."

"Why?" I growl. "Do you really have to ask that? Thanks to you, Mom didn't know I existed! The two of you went away for whole days. Into the hospital, out of the hospital. I was ten years old, Dylan, ten! You stayed away for entire weekends and I had to cook for myself, do the laundry, and change your stinking sweaty sheets. Whenever Mom came back, she was always mad at me. She snarled at me, told me I had to try harder. After all, it wasn't my little brother's fault that he was sick. Everything at home revolved around you. Everything!"

Dylan's eyes filled with tears. "Do you think it's what I wanted?"

I snort. Even after all these years, he still can't stop playing the victim.

"You stayed in bed and Mom took care of you. She was with you every day, but she'd stopped caring about me. I got thrown out. She rejected me, like I didn't belong to her. And she let you go on living there. You always came first."

DYLAN

Kelly's words go through me like bullets.

"Be glad!" I scream. "Be glad she didn't choose you!"

Kelly's eyebrows go up. His Fright Night makeup moves stiffly.

"When are you going to get it? I didn't want her to take care of me."

Behind me, I hear Sofia and Quin coming into the bunker. Sandy grabs his knife and holds it out.

"Get back."

I'm shocked by the sharp blade. Is that what Sandy used to carve up Martin's face?

"You're acting like you're the victim here!" yells Sandy. "But you grew up with your mom. You have no idea what Kelly went through because of you!"

"Is that why you wanted to kill me?" I ask quietly.

Kelly looks at me. "What?"

"This postcard." I take it out of my pocket and hold it up. "You recognize this place, don't you?"

It was the last vacation for the three of us. Mom left me alone for two weeks and I hung out with Kelly, building forts, eating ice cream, and swimming all day long. It felt like I finally had a big brother.

But back home it began all over again. Mom moaned that I'd spent way too much time in the sun. Dr. Luiting was never going to believe I was sick. So she forced me to rest in bed again, and Kelly retreated to the attic. He went back to being distant and mean. Within a few weeks, it was like the vacation had never happened.

"Here." I turn the card to show him the words. "You want to kill me."

Kelly's expression freezes. "I didn't write that."

I hold out the card farther. "Well, you're the only one who knows where we went on vacation that time."

"That's not true. I told Sandy . . ." Kelly turns to look at Sandy, who's blinking his yellow eyes way too quickly. "Sandy? Did you . . ."

"What if I did?"

Kelly stares at Sandy in disbelief. "You threatened to kill my brother?"

"That thing!" Sandy's trembling fingers grip the handle of the knife more tightly. "That's not your brother! I'm your brother. I'm the one who's been here for you all these years!"

Kelly slowly shakes his head. "When did you send the card?"

"Monday."

"So that's why you were back so late from the grocery store." Kelly's voice cracks. "Why?"

"I wanted to terrify him. Then he could feel what it's like for once. Someone had to do it, didn't they?"

"Your plan didn't work," I say. "I don't live there anymore."

Kelly and Sandy both look up at the same time.

"I live with Quin now."

Kelly's eyes widen. "What? Why?"

"Because it was too dangerous at home."

Sandy takes a step forward. "That mouth of your just spits out lies."

And then everything happens at once. He grabs Sofia, holds the knife to her throat, and pulls her away from us.

"What are you doing?!" Quin and I both shoot forward.

"Don't move!"

"Let her go," I say. "She has nothing to do with this."

Sandy shakes his head. "Not until you say sorry."

I look at Sofia, who's clutching Sandy's arm. If anything happens to her tonight, I'll never forgive myself.

"S-sorry," I say quickly. "Sorry."

"Not to me. To *him*!"

I look at Kelly, who can't take his eyes off Sofia and the knife. He looks lost, his arms dangling limply beside his body.

"I'm sorry," I say to him.

"And now *mean it*!" Sandy presses the knife harder into Sofia's throat. I see the tension increasing under the blade. Any more and she'll start bleeding . . .

"I really mean it!" I scream. "Let her go. Please!"

"I think someone's in love." Sandy bursts out laughing. "Mommy's boy has a crush!"

Mommy's boy.

Inside my head, something snaps.

"I am not a mommy's boy!" I take a step toward Kelly. "You didn't listen to me that afternoon. I tried to tell you. I had to pretend I was sick. Mom made me."

Now it's perfectly silent in the bunker. Sandy loosens his grip on Sofia's neck. I can feel Quin staring at me in shock, but I don't care. I have to tell the truth.

For Kelly, and for me.

"It was Mom who pushed me down the stairs that afternoon."

The words are out of my mouth—and it seems like they're only really sinking in to me now. That must be what happened. How else did Mom come running downstairs? She must have forgotten something and come back. Then she heard the fight between me and Kelly. Just before I tripped, I felt something on my back. Mom's hands.

"Mom made me sick, and I had to play along. At the hospital, with my friends, with my teacher at school, with you. If I didn't do as she said, she hit me."

"But . . ." I can see that Kelly doesn't believe me, but at the same time he knows I'm not making this up. "It was me. Mom said I'd made you fall."

"But how?" I yell. "You were upstairs!"

"I upset you. I scared you so much that you lost your balance. I was dangerous."

I can feel tears burning in my eyes. How can he have believed what Mom said? Has he been going around all these years thinking that my leg was his fault?

But Mom did exactly the same to me. She made me believe that I was really sick, that I was going to die. There were times

I hardly dared to go to sleep, because I was scared I wouldn't wake up.

"You weren't dangerous," I say quietly. "Mom was the only dangerous one in the house."

"How . . ." Kelly looks at me, then Quin, and then back again. "How did you get away?"

"Dylan?"

I look up, straight into Eliza's sparkling eyes. What is she doing here? This is a completely different hospital!

"Fancy running into you here!" Eliza comes and sits beside me. "How are you doing?"

I fidget on the plastic chair in the waiting room. What should I say? Mom could come back from her conversation with Dr. Luiting at any minute.

"Yeah, I'm good."

"Are you here alone?"

"No." I look at the door along the corridor. "Mom's in with the doctor."

Eliza follows my gaze. "With Dr. Luiting?"

Is that strange? My hands are sweating.

"Yes . . ."

"What's wrong with your leg?"

I take hold of it and shift it a little. "I, um, I fell."

"Dylan!" Mom comes hurrying down the corridor in her high heels. "Is everything okay?"

Then she sees Eliza, and her eyes widen. "Dr. Savory?"

"Hello, Mrs. Dumont." Eliza stands up and shakes Mom's hand. "I was just having a little chat with Dylan. He was telling me about his accident."

"Accident?" Mom looks at my leg and makes a careless gesture. "Oh yes, of course. The accident."

Something flashes across Eliza's face, and the sparkle goes out for a second.

"Okay, then. I'd better be off. Bye, Dylan." She gives me a little wave. "See you."

"Eliza was on to me. Or actually she was on to Mom. She asked to see all my files and then she discussed the situation with Dr. Luiting. He'd been working on all kinds of new tests for a couple of years by then."

I can see that my story is slowly getting through to Kelly. Sandy is still glaring at me. I can't stop talking now. I have to make sure that Sandy lets Sofia go.

"They reported it to social services. One night they just turned up at the door unannounced. They did that so Mom wouldn't have time to"—my breath catches—"do anything to hurt me."

Quin curses. Now he knows the whole truth. All that time he knew Mom had gone crazy, but he had no idea that it was aimed at me.

There's nothing holding me back now. My whole story can be out there. Kelly has to know the truth. I wasn't Mom's favorite. I was just her favorite plaything. A doll she could make sick so she'd get attention from doctors. Whenever Dr. Luiting paid her a compliment, she glowed with pride. Gerda, the concerned neighbor, was a gift. No one realized what Mom was really like when my bedroom curtains were closed. No one except for Eliza.

Dr. Savory.

Dr. Savior.

"Here." I pull the photo of Kelly and Mom out of my pocket. "This is for you."

Kelly takes it from me. "How did you get this?"

"It was on the windowsill all that time. Mom removed everything else to do with you. If I asked about you, she hit me. So I taught myself to forget you."

Kelly looks at me. "So it really was Mom?"

I feel Mom's hands on my back again. I see the eager look in her eyes when she came running down the stairs and saw my injured leg. She thought it was awesome that I actually had something wrong with me. Just as long as I wasn't happy or healthy.

"Yes."

Kelly's eyes fill with tears. "I should have protected you."

"That's enough!" Sandy shoves Sofia aside. Quin immediately pulls her out of his reach.

"He's lying, Kelly!" Sandy's face flushes red. I can see it right through his makeup. "Are you falling for it again? You can't trust anyone—get that into your head! Everyone's out to destroy us. Social services, Nell, your mom, my mom, him." Sandy points the knife and runs at full speed toward me.

SOFIA

"No!" My scream echoes off the four walls of the bunker. Not Dylan, that can't happen, that mustn't happen.

Dylan's eyes widen. I gasp for breath. But I don't see what's happened until Sandy steps aside. That razor-sharp knife, the knife that was just at my throat, is stuck in Kelly's chest, right up to the handle.

He'd jumped between them.

Everyone steps back, except for Dylan, who kneels down next to his brother.

"Kelly!" Dylan takes hold of the knife handle, but then lets go. There's a pool of blood forming around the blade. "Someone do something!"

All three of us stare at the scene in front of us, but no one moves.

"The walkie-talkie . . ." Dylan reaches into the inside pocket of Kelly's costume. "How do these things work? How does it work?"

Finally the walkie-talkie turns on.

"Hello?" says a tinny voice.

"Help! My brother's dying. We need help!"

"What? Where are you?"

"In the bunker . . . I . . ." Dylan takes Kelly's hand and makes him sit up. "Kelly, please."

But Kelly's eyes are rolling back. A dark puddle trickles out from under his body. I lean my whole weight back against the wall, like I might be able to disappear into it.

"The bunker?" the voice says. Someone yells something in the background. "We know where you are. We're calling an ambulance. Okay?"

Dylan throws away the walkie-talkie and pulls Kelly toward him, who hangs limply in his arms. "What have you gone and done?" The dark puddle on the ground grows bigger and bigger. That's way too much blood. "You're my brother, Kelly, Kelly. You always have been." Dylan lays Kelly down and starts frantically scratching at his brother's face. "I need to get this makeup off. I want to see my brother!"

Quin and I kneel down beside him and help. The makeup has hardened and it comes off Kelly's cheeks in chunks. Slowly but surely, his own skin appears, pale and fragile.

Kelly's eyes open. For a moment, he stares at Dylan. His lips barely move when he whispers, "It's okay."

Then his eyes roll back in his head again. All I can see is the whites.

"Kelly, stay with me!"

"He can't hear you." Behind us, Sandy has taken off his wig. "He's—"

"Shut your mouth!" Dylan's still brushing the makeup off Kelly's face. "Kelly, can you hear me? Help's going to be here any minute. Just hang on a bit longer."

MURDERER?

I know I wasn't the one who stuck the knife into you.
I was the one the knife was meant for.

But I still murdered you.
I murdered you by forgetting you.

Because if I'd fought harder,
for myself and for you,
then you'd still be alive.

AFTER FRIGHT NIGHT

SOFIA

The back doors of the ambulance are open and the morning sun is peeping through the trees.

The EMT lays a hand on my shoulder. "It might leave a small scar."

I nod numbly. What does that matter?

"Your parents are on their way." The man gives me a pat on the shoulder. "You just sit here and wait."

I pull the blanket he gave me more tightly around me. It's not cold, but it feels safer that way.

Quin comes and sits beside me. Although he doesn't have any injuries, the ambulance crew still wanted to check him out. They gave him a blanket, too, which is hanging loosely around his shoulders. Together we watch the flashing lights of the police car. Two men are leading Sandy away.

"I didn't mean to!" I hear him shouting. "I didn't! He jumped in the way, and—"

One of the cops pushes Sandy into the car and the rest of his words are lost behind the closed door. Curious Fright Nighters and journalists, who have come flocking, are taking photos from behind the barriers. The police car drives away without sirens, as if they hope to erase Sandy by silence.

Quin doesn't say anything. For the first time since I've known him, he has nothing to say. Dylan's sitting a short distance away. He has a blanket, too, but his looks twice as big as ours. He's hanging his head and barely reacting to the police officer's questions.

I hear the wheels of a gurney. The black bag lying on it says it all. A ripple runs through the crowd, and the photographers start clicking away.

When the bag was zipped up, Dylan broke. I've never heard anyone make such an animal sound as he did. I know there'll be nights when I hear that scream all over again.

Quin and I watch as the gurney with Kelly on it is lifted into the other ambulance.

The back doors close with a bang. I look at Dylan again. For a moment, our gazes meet and I see his dark-brown eyes. The same eyes as his brother, with the same pain. I hold up my wrist and point at my bracelet.

Everything will be fine, I think. *In the end.*

Dylan nods. It's a small nod, but I think he understands.

I feel a hand on my shoulder again. When I look up, I see Nell standing there. Her mascara has left dark rings under her eyes, but otherwise she's as pale as a ghost.

"I just wanted to let you know we're going to the hospital."

Quin and I quickly stand up to let Martin past. He has a white bandage around his arm and my bloodstained denim jacket in his hand.

When he holds it out to me, I shake my head. Like I'll ever wear that thing again.

"Just throw it away somewhere, please."

He nods. "Will do."

"Good luck," says Nell. She takes my hands and gives them a squeeze. The smile she gives me seems to be hard work. "With everything."

"You guys too," I say.

Quin and I watch as the second ambulance drives away. I pull the blanket even more tightly around me.

Quin nudges me. "Where's Dylan?"

I turn around. The spot where Dylan was sitting just now is empty. I look around the crowd, but I don't see him anywhere.

More cars come along. I recognize my mom and dad's and Quin's parents' too. When Mom gets out, a shock goes through me.

"Ah, of course."

"What?" asks Quin.

I look at him. "It's Sunday."

DYLAN

"I need to pee."

The police officer stops her rapid-fire questions and gives me a searching look. Then she nods. "Sure. The restrooms are over there. Come straight back, though. We have more questions for you."

I stand up and walk toward the building. When I turn around, I see the cop talking to one of her colleagues. I throw the blanket off my shoulders and run to the bikes.

...

In the morning, the building looks whiter than ever. The sunlight glints off the windows on the first floor, almost blinding me. The revolving door isn't moving yet. Visiting hours don't start for a while yet.

I leave my bike in the rack and walk up to the entrance. Inside, the staff members are going about their business.

"You're early." An older woman with a walker comes to stand next to me. "I thought I was the only fanatic."

I nod.

"Come sit with me, young man." The woman slowly sinks down onto a bench. As I sit beside her, she gives a deep sigh.

"I always dread this. Every time. But he's still my son. They often let me in earlier, so I have an extra hour."

I look at the revolving door, which still hasn't moved.

"Can you keep a little secret?"

I'm sick of secrets, but still I nod.

"Sometimes I play hooky." The woman smiles. "Then I go to the beach and I eat fish."

A smile bubbles up inside me.

"But then I feel guilty. On Sundays I should be here. I'd give my life if it would make my son better."

The smile turns into a lump. A brick. I touch the broken glasses in my pocket.

"Are you okay?" The woman sounds worried.

I nod, but suddenly tears are running down my cheeks.

"Here." She hands me an old-fashioned embroidered hand-kerchief. "Don't worry. It's clean."

I rub my eyes with the handkerchief, but they fill right back up. The revolving door turns and a woman comes out. She's wearing a white uniform and I recognize her from the visiting hours.

"Mrs. Van Diepenhoven?"

"That's me. Have a nice day, young man." The woman struggles to her feet and looks up at the sky. "It's beautiful weather for a day at the beach."

I watch her walking to the entrance, with her bent back

and her shuffling feet. The nurse helps her inside and then I'm alone again.

Mom's probably eating breakfast now. I can picture her in the chair by the window. If she makes an effort, she can see me from there, but she won't.

I'd give my life if it would make my son better.

I can feel the blood rushing through my veins. I think of the look in Sofia's eyes when I ate the cockroach for her. I'd give my life for her too. I bet Quin will be going on about that again before long. He'll give me a little break, but then it'll start again. Everything will eventually go back to the way it was.

But maybe better.

Because I owe that to Kelly. From now on, every day of my life has to be an A+ day.

The revolving door slowly comes to a stop. Does Mom know yet that she just lost a son? Does she care? She's probably more interested in her new wheelchair, which she's had for a few weeks now. Her legs are sick, she says.

I close my eyes for a moment and let the sun warm me. Hester's making lasagna tonight, my favorite. She does that every Sunday, because she knows what kind of day it is. There'll be a plate for me, because I'm part of the family. Maybe Quin was right. Maybe it's always been that way.

I stand up. It's time.

A few seconds later, I'm back at my bike and swinging my leg over the seat. I take one last look at the white building and feel the sun on my face.

She's right. It's beautiful weather for a day at the beach.

MAREN STOFFELS
ON *FRIGHT NIGHT*

One summer break, I took part in a Fright Night in the woods, without knowing exactly what I had let myself in for. I was terrified. All those actors leaping out of the bushes with chainsaws, fake blood, and layers of makeup on their faces.

No, Fright Night was definitely not for me.

But I couldn't help being fascinated by the subject. Why would anyone want to take part in such an experience? A story came into my head, and it started with Dylan. Because he has a very unusual fear: his mother.

For every book I write, I make sure that the story is realistic, so for this story I got in touch with Nina. She survived the form of child abuse that Dylan had to deal with. It's known as Munchausen syndrome by proxy (MSBP).

Nina was made sick by her own mother for fourteen years, so that her mother would receive attention from doctors and hospitals. Nina helped me a lot by telling me her story. As a writer, I was able to craft that information into a new story: Dylan's.

Do you recognize yourself (or someone else) in Dylan? You can always phone the Childhelp National Child Abuse Hotline at 1-800-4-A-CHILD (1-800-422-4453). Or visit them online at childhelp.org.

DON'T MISS ANOTHER NAIL-BITING READ FROM UNDERLINED

I can see It from here.
It can't see me.
It has to pay.
For everything.
All I need is a sign.
Please.
Give me a sign that I can begin.

MINT

"He's gay. For sure." Sky's sitting on the backrest of the bench, right behind Alissa and me. It's just the three of us. The rest of the park is deserted.

"Don't think so." Alissa takes out her wallet. "How much do you want to bet?"

I have no idea who my two best friends are talking about. Their conversations often pass me by, like I'm on the other side of a wall.

Alissa waves a five-dollar bill around. It reminds me of the first day of junior high. I thought Alissa had made a bet then too.

She came up to my desk that first morning and asked if the seat next to me was taken. Alissa was the kind of girl who could have sat anywhere. She was so incredibly beautiful. Her eyes were the color of the sea on the Italian coast, where I'd spent the summer. I looked around suspiciously. Where were her giggling friends, laughing at me from a distance because I'd fallen for it?

But there was no one else there. We were the only ones in the classroom.

Sky's voice brings me back to the present. "Let's bet for a pizza," he says. "And Miles can deliver it. Perfect."

So they're talking about Miles, who works at the pizzeria with Sky. I've never seen him before, but Alissa's mentioned him a few times.

A girl with blond hair and a red scarf around her neck comes jogging into the park. As she passes us, she flashes me a quick smile.

"He's on his way, so now we just have to wait and see." Sky puts his phone in his pocket and casually rolls a cigarette. He never has actual packs of cigarettes. Sky always does everything just a little bit differently from everyone else.

"Did it hurt?" I hear Alissa ask. I'm back on the bench in the park. What were they talking about now?

I follow Alissa's gaze to Sky's eyebrow piercing, which he had done a while ago. When he turned up at school the next day, the skin around the piercing was red and swollen. I touch my own eyebrow, which also hurt for a few days.

At first I thought it was a coincidence, but then when Alissa broke her wrist in gym, mine was painful for weeks too.

Can I feel other people's pain? Is that possible? It feels supernatural, weird. And if anyone finds out, I'll get even more of a reputation for being crazy.

Sky points at his eyebrow. "So much gunk came out! I could have made it into a smoothie."

Alissa gives him a shove and he nearly falls off the back of the bench. "Stop! You're going to scare me out of it."

Since when has Alissa wanted a piercing? I try to imagine what it would look like on her, a little ring through her eyebrow.

A couple weeks ago in Textile Studies, we had to make

dresses out of garbage bags. Alissa pulled hers over her head, grabbed hold of it on one side, and shot a staple through the plastic. Then she paraded around the classroom like she was on a catwalk. Some of the boys started whistling. Even in a garbage bag, she was stunning.

"Where's that pizza?" Alissa asks impatiently.

"Miles has half an hour to get here. After that, the pizza's free."

A few minutes later, a scooter with a big blue trunk on the back drives into the park.

Sky grabs my wrist and looks at my watch. "Bang on time. Typical Miles. You see? He's a punctual gay guy."

My stomach's churning, like I'm about to take an important exam.

"Stop it." Alissa quickly straightens her T-shirt. It's a small gesture, but I can tell she's nervous.

Miles brakes in front of our bench and gives Sky a wave. When he lifts the visor of his helmet, I see two bright-blue eyes, like Alissa's. But there's something cold about these eyes. They have nothing to do with the Italian sea, but are more like icy water. I get a weird feeling that I can't quite identify.

"One pepperoni pizza?" The boy takes out a pizza box. The scent of melted cheese makes my mouth water.

"Yep. It's for us." Then Sky points at Alissa. "She's paying."

"You think?" Alissa looks at the boy. "Hey, Miles."

MILES

I don't like it when people know my name and I don't know theirs. Feels like I'm down 1–0.

I've seen this girl before. She meets Sky after work sometimes. I noticed her immediately because she has the same blue eyes as me. Dad used to say I was the only one except him with blue peepers like this, but he was wrong. This girl's eyes are hypnotic.

Did Sky tell her my name?

The girl smiles. "Want a slice?"

I hesitate, because I really need to get going, but something about her voice makes me stop.

It's only then that I notice the other girl on the bench. She's leaning forward slightly, with her straight hair hanging over her face like two curtains. She doesn't quite seem to belong.

"It's almost time for your break, isn't it? Come on, have some." Seems the girl with the blue eyes knows not just my name, but my work schedule too.

I can see part of her bare neck.

What would it feel like to kiss that soft bit of skin?

I'm startled by my own thought. After Karla, I made up my mind never to feel anything for a girl again. It's easier to reject them all than to let anyone get close. Because when they get close, they start asking questions. Questions I can't answer.

I know I should go, but somehow I find myself taking off my helmet and sitting down beside her.

"Here." The pretty girl passes me the box. As I eat my slice, I dare to sneak a closer look at her. There has to be something about her that's disappointing, something that'll help me to forget about her later.

But her voice sounds like she's singing. Her eyes are an endless blue. And she smells like autumn sunshine.

I'm not sure I want to forget her.

I swallow the pizza. "And who are you?"

ALISSA

We're sitting so close that Miles's leg is touching mine. He's looking at me as if he hopes to find something in my face. His eyes scan every inch of my skin.

I've never talked to Miles, but whenever I go to meet Sky at work, I watch him from a distance.

Miles stands out, not because he's good-looking, but because he doesn't seem to want to be. It's as if his looks torment him somehow. And that's something I recognize.

Boys like to check me out, and it drives me crazy. Andreas is the last boy I kissed, and I really did like him. But after our kiss, I heard him bragging about it like I wasn't even a person, just some "hot" girl.

Sky's handsome too, but his rough-and-tough exterior scares a lot of people off. Which seems like a great idea to me.

At home, I sometimes stare at myself in the mirror. I don't dare get a tattoo, but how about a piercing? Once I put a dot on the side of my nose with a Sharpie. The thought of a stud in my nose instantly made me feel stronger.

"And who are you?" asks Miles.

"Alissa."

"Are you gay?" Sky asks.

I get why the teachers say he's direct. He's like a bulldozer sometimes.

Miles shakes his head irritably. "No, I'm not gay."

Sky lights his cigarette. "No need to get pissed. Gay people are cool."

Miles puts the last bit of pizza into his mouth and stands up. "Got to go."

Is he leaving because Sky asked that question? I realize that I'm riled up. I want Miles to look at me again the way he just did. It was like he could see much more than my exterior.

"Sky's paying for the pizza," I say. "And the tip."

SKY

I curse to myself.

Alissa likes him.

I thought this was just about a bet, but Alissa smiled at Miles the way only she can. Her boy-slaying smile.

When I get home, I turn the amp for my electric drum kit up high. Drumming always works, but not this time. Even after playing for half an hour, I still feel angry. I pull off my headphones.

Why can't I shake it off?

Alissa doesn't have a clue that I only started dating Caitlin to divert attention.

Caitlin's in our year at school. If I squint, they even look a bit like each other. But Caitlin's blue eyes don't match up to the real thing.

I fall back onto my bed and look at the group photo on my nightstand. Having it there makes it hard for me to sleep, but it's even harder without it.

I pick up the photo and hold it close to my face. There's a small worn patch where I sometimes press my lips to it. We're standing close together, our arms touching.

I'd really like to cut everyone else out of the photo, but this way Alissa can come into my room without realizing what's up. There's no need to worry about Mint. She spends half her time floating in another dimension.

"You belong with me," I say quietly to the photo. "You just need to see it."

MILES

Alissa. Every pizza I deliver for the rest of the evening, I'm thinking about her. As I ride my scooter home, I can still see her bare neck.

I don't realize where I am until I'm almost at the front door. This is my old street.

How is that possible? All this time, I've never gone the wrong way. I settled into our new place immediately.

My heart skips a beat when I see that nothing's changed. The sidewalk is lower in one place, where I could always ride over it on my bike without bumping the back wheel.

In the window of number 39, there's still a line of wooden cows on the ledge. I used to spend ages looking at them when I was a little kid. Dad stood patiently beside me as I counted them and gave them all names.

The memory's painful.

Nothing's changed here, and yet *everything* has changed.

SKY

On Friday afternoon, I'm happy when I can finally leave school. I know I shouldn't be mad at Alissa, but I still am.

She's in love with the wrong person. Why can't she see that?

I head into the employees-only section at the pizzeria and, as I'm putting on my apron, I spot a flyer on the table.

Curious, I read the words.

SUPER-REALISTIC ESCAPE ROOM!
THE HAPPY FAMILY

THE DOOR SHUTS.
YOU HAVE SIXTY MINUTES.
BUT WHERE WILL YOU START LOOKING?

FIND THE CLUES! CRACK THE CODES! SOLVE THE PUZZLES!
CAN YOU ESCAPE WITHIN AN HOUR?

BUT BE WARNED:
THIS IS NERVE-RACKING, BLOOD-CHILLING, HEART-STOPPING!
NOT FOR THE FAINT OF HEART OR THE FEEBLE OF BRAIN!

THE HAPPY FAMILY IS DESIGNED FOR GROUPS OF AT LEAST 4 PEOPLE.
(THIS ESCAPE ROOM IS TERRIFYINGLY TENSE!)

I read the flyer three times to let it all sink in. The word "super-realistic" has sucked me in. I always think the haunted houses at the county fair are ridiculously fake, but this? This is something I have to do.

Maybe, just maybe, just for a moment, I'll forget the photo on my nightstand when I'm in this Escape Room. And maybe I'll forget that those blue eyes will never look at me the way I want them to.

"Shouldn't you be working?"

I turn around and see Miles. He points at the flyer in my hand. "What's that?"

I'm mad at him too, maybe even more than I am at Alissa. Those longing looks he was giving her yesterday. I just can't bring myself to look at Caitlin that way, no matter how hard I try.

I stuff the flyer into my jeans pocket. "Nothing."

Alissa and Mint are waiting outside when I leave work later. Alissa's piercing twinkles away at me. Like she wasn't pretty enough already.

"You coming to the movie?" Alissa asks.

"Got a date with Caitlin." The moment I say it, I feel nervous again. Recently I've had the feeling that Caitlin wants to go further than just kissing. I know I should want the same, but I can't do it. My mind's on someone else.

"Things are pretty serious with you two, huh?"

I make a strange noise that could mean anything. A quick change of subject.

"Want to go here next Friday?" I pull the flyer for the Escape Room out of my pocket.

Alissa frowns. "What is it?"

"Oh, I've heard about that!" To my surprise, Mint pulls the leaflet out of my hand. "You have to solve puzzles so you can escape."

"And that's your idea of fun?" Alissa raises an eyebrow.

Mint nods. "Sounds cool."

Alissa exchanges a quick glance with me. She's clearly thinking the same thing I am: Mint's too timid to do anything. She usually stays at home when we have a school trip, and Alissa and I go to the fair on our own every year because Mint says the rides make her nauseous. She rarely visits me at work, always claiming she has a stomachache or headache.

"Fine by me," Alissa says.

I point to the bottom half of the flyer. "We just need a fourth person."

"Caitlin?" Mint suggests.

Being with Caitlin already feels like one big real-life Escape Room.

"Or Miles?" Alissa says.

I curse to myself. No way I want to spend sixty minutes watching those two getting closer.

"Then there'll be four of us." Alissa looks at me. "Shall I ask him?"